A IS FOR ABIGAIL

SHORT FICTION, INSPIRED BY LIFE

SIXPENNY CROSS - LARGE PRINT
BOOK ONE

VICTORIA TWEAD
NEW YORK TIMES BESTSELLING AUTHOR

Ant Press
Large Print
Edition

CONTENTS

A IS FOR ABIGAIL

SIXPENNY CROSS 1

Abigail Martin has everything: beauty, money, a loving husband, and a fabulous house in the village of Sixpenny Cross. But Abigail is denied the one thing she craves... A baby.

1

I'm old now. My hair is the colour of the ashes in the fire and my skin is no longer smooth and tight like yours. But although my voice quavers when I speak, I still feel young in my head.

Like you, I was born in the village of Sixpenny Cross. Now, eighty years later, I'm still here. I've watched new families arrive, and old ones die out. I've seen babies born and watched them grow into adults. So many stories!

Sometimes I don't sleep so well because memories crowd into my head.

But you, little one, with your soft golden curls, you are asleep now, but I'll tell you a story while I watch over you. It's hard to choose which tale to tell first.

A is for Abigail. Yes, I'll tell you about Abigail Martin.

When I saw the travelling people drive through the village this spring, heading for Sixpenny Woods, I was reminded of nice, young Abigail Martin.

Poor Abigail had a deep yearning, a hollow part in her soul. I am sure it was because of that terrible need, that great gnawing emptiness she felt inside, that she made a bargain.

And twenty-four hours later, when she heard that tiny snuffling sound, she could have ignored it.

But she didn't.

And life for Abigail was never the same again.

2

"It isn't fair, Daisy," Abigail complained. She began counting off points on her manicured fingers. "Look at me! I have naturally blonde hair. (Well, almost.) I'm happily married and I live in a great big, beautiful house. Sixpenny Cross won the Prettiest Village in England contest three years running. I'm not short of money and I don't need to work. I have friends. I even have you, Sam."

She reached forward to fondle the retriever's golden ears. Sam's brown eyes stared into Abigail's green ones.

"Oh come on, Abigail, cheer up!" said Daisy, setting down her coffee cup. "It's really not like you to moan so much. You should be grateful for all your blessings."

"I have a sister with three children," Abigail continued, ignoring her friend. "And a brother with two. I even volunteer at the school so I'm *surrounded* by children."

"Listen, you can always adopt."

"I told you, Aiden won't even entertain the idea. He says he could never love a child that wasn't his."

She broke off to stare through the window. In the distance an old lady, a shawl thrown over hunched shoulders, trudged along a lane, dragging a small child by the hand. Travellers.

"How long are the gypsies going to stay in Sixpenny Woods?" asked Daisy, following her gaze. "You know our lawnmower went missing last week? Simon is positive it was the gypsies."

"I expect they'll move on soon. They always do."

"Look at the time!" exclaimed Daisy. "I promised Simon I'd cook steak for supper tonight. I'd better hurry or there'll be nothing left at the butcher's."

She gathered her stuff, kissed her friend on the cheek and headed for the door.

"Now stop feeling sorry for yourself, Abigail. It'll happen when you least expect it."

"Will it?" Abigail asked Sam as Daisy closed the back door behind herself. "Will it really? Will it *ever* happen? Aiden and I have been married nearly five years. We hardly see each other because of his job. And how many children do we have? None!"

Aiden stared out at the iconic skyline. The hotel room was expensive, a penthouse commanding a spectacular view of London's most famous landmarks. He could even see the silver-grey Thames threading through the city. Behind him, a woman was dressing.

"Help me with this zipper, would you?" she said, her accent unmistakably American.

She stepped forward and stood with her back to him, blocking his panoramic view. Even though she no longer attracted him, he couldn't help admiring her shapely curves.

She was perfectly aware of the effect she had on men and unhurriedly lifted her long hair to allow him access to the fastenings. Aiden zipped, then battled with a tiny pearl button.

"There you go," he said. "Nice dress."

"It wasn't cheap. So little choice. The stores here are nothing like back home. So *rural*. Gee, I'll be glad when I get out of this grey country."

"It won't be long now."

"Okay, I'm going out for a couple of hours. I'll see you later."

She stepped away, and Aiden's view of London sprang back. But it wasn't London or Martha he was thinking about. It was Abigail and Sixpenny Cross.

Abigail sat in the kitchen, deep in thought. In the background, a newscaster on the radio relayed news of the Falklands war, but she was deaf to it all.

"*Whoof.*"

Sam expectantly eyed the leash that

dangled from the hook on the back of the kitchen door.

The phone rang and Abigail picked up the kitchen extension, switching off the radio and Margaret Thatcher at the same time. Sam lost hope and flopped onto the floor.

"Abigail?"

"Oh, hi Hilary, how are you?"

"Abigail, I'm sorry to 'ave to do this to you at such short notice…"

"What's up, Hilary? You sound stressed."

Hilary was the Martins' cleaning lady.

"It's my older sister in Wales. She's 'ad a fall, poor thing, a serious one. I'm going to 'ave to go up there and 'elp out. I 'ate letting you down, but…"

"Oh Hilary! How awful! Of course you must go! Don't worry about me, I'll be absolutely fine. You know it's just Sam and me in the house and it hardly gets dirty."

"Are you sure?"

"Of course I'm sure! This house is much too big for Aiden and me, most of it is never used. It just won't be a problem." She paused, and then added quickly, "Of course your job will be waiting for you when you get back."

"Thank you, if you are absolutely sure…" There was relief in Hilary's voice.

"Don't worry about a thing, just go to your sister. I do hope she gets well soon, and I'll see you when you come back."

Abigail sighed as she rang off.

"Okay, time for your walk, boy."

Sam jumped up and danced round the kitchen, his eyes never leaving the leash on the back door.

The phone rang again.

Sam flopped down on the floor once more, his head on his paws.

Abigail picked up the receiver, convinced it would be Hilary again, but it wasn't her cleaning lady this time.

"Abs?"

"Hi Aiden, how's things?"

Aiden phoned daily, and she loved the opportunity to chat. If only he had more time.

"Good, good."

"Job going well?"

"Yes, we're really close to getting that contract, just a few loose ends to tie up with the client."

"I'll be glad when they finally sign. This has been going on for so long. Are you still coming home on Friday?"

"Of course I am, Abs. I can't wait!"

"I miss you so much, Aiden."

"I know… But I'll be home soon. Any village news?"

"No, not really. Hilary phoned to say she's gone to Wales so won't be cleaning for us for a while. Her sister had a fall. And Daisy came round for coffee. That's it really."

"Well, we'll be able to catch up properly on Friday evening. Oh, must go, my client is here. Bye Abs, love you."

The phone went dead and Abigail sighed. Sam opened one eye hopefully.

"It's your turn now," she said, clipping the leash to his collar.

Locking the door behind her, Abigail and Sam set off down the path for their walk, their legs brushing the daffodils that leaned towards them.

Turn left or right? Which way along the lane? Sam faced right, straining the leash, hoping Sixpenny Woods and its wealth of scents would be today's destination.

"Sorry, Sam, but all the time the travellers are camped in the woods, we're not going there. We'd better turn left and walk to the village."

Abigail tugged Sam the other way and together they headed along the lane in the direction of the village. Sam snuffled happily in the lush grass, reading messages left by rabbits and other animals. Abigail watched a newborn lamb in the field trying out its legs as it danced around its grazing mother before butting its hard little head against her side, begging for a drink.

In the distance, she could see a tractor gouging neat parallel lines in the soil. She guessed it was Archie Draper, and waved. But Archie was too busy concentrating on ploughing straight lines to notice her.

It should have been idyllic, and it was. Except... Except for the hollowness inside Abigail. A deep, dark hole of cold nothingness that only a baby could fill.

3

The expensive Harley Street specialist said there was nothing wrong. He had pronounced Abigail fit and well. There was nothing wrong with Aiden either. But still no baby appeared.

Abigail tried to put the whole painful subject out of her mind.

"Hello, Stan," she said as a familiar figure pedalled past her.

"Afternoon, Mrs Martin. Lovely day!"

Crime in Sixpenny Cross was almost non-existent and for years Stan Cooper had been the village police officer. Unless it was urgent, he travelled everywhere on his bicycle. In an emergency, he used the police car which had become a fixture in front of the police station.

Aiden always said that Stan had the easiest job in Sixpenny Cross and the only job he could think of that was easier than Stan's was being a weather forecaster in the Sahara Desert. It was probably a good thing that Sixpenny Cross wasn't gripped by a crime wave. Although Stan was a well-liked and diligent policeman, his clumsiness was legendary.

"Did you find Daisy and Simon's lawnmower?" she called after him.

"Yes, they forgot they lent it out to Frank Jones."

"Not stolen then?"

"No!" Stan shouted over his shoulder, wobbled dangerously, righted himself and pedalled away.

Abigail and Aiden's house was half a mile from the village green. They'd found it in the glossy pages of *Country Estates,* a magazine they subscribed to when they lived in London. Abigail had fallen in love with the house even before they viewed it. It had a hefty price tag, but for such a beautiful house, with its extensive grounds and separate guest cottage, what did one expect?

And they could afford it. They could also afford to pay for a cleaning lady and gardener. Abigail's plan was that she'd soon fill the house with children who would play in the grounds and attend the village school. But the house remained scarcely lived in. With Aiden away so much, Abigail used only the kitchen, sunroom, bedroom and bathroom.

Higgledy-piggledy cottages, some thatched, some with red roof-tiles, lined the approach to the village. Yellow daffodils swayed in the spring sunshine and bees were already busy visiting the flowers, one by one. Here the road was better, and there was a pavement to walk on.

The Dew Drop Inn was quiet. Angus McDonald, the landlord, was busy sweeping the floor and didn't see Abigail pass.

Abigail passed the little school, listening to the hum of learning. She glanced at her Tiffany watch. Soon the bell would ring and the children would spill out into the yard.

One day, maybe, her own children would be among them.

At the centre of Sixpenny Cross was the large village green. In summer, cricket matches took place against rival village teams. There was a pond fringed by reeds, and a willow tree that trailed branches into the water and shaded a bench where old folks liked to sit.

Today the green was empty apart from a pair of mallard ducks guarding an untidy nest. Cars were slowly arriving and mothers were beginning to migrate towards the school, preparing to collect their youngsters. Abigail greeted a few that she knew by sight.

At the village shop, which was also the Post Office, Jayne Fairweather, the postmistress, waved to her as she passed.

"Hello, Abigail!" she called. "Is your husband coming home soon?"

"Yes, this weekend!"

It was good to be known and to exchange friendly words with fellow villagers, but Abigail had never felt wholly accepted. She was very aware that many of the villagers' families went back generations. The headstones in the churchyard were proof of that. Abigail and Aiden would always be 'newcomers'. However friendly people seemed to be, they'd still give her sidelong glances when they thought she wasn't looking.

When she'd mentioned it to Aiden, he'd shrugged.

"They're just jealous," he said.

"Jealous of what?"

"Our money, probably."

The irony of it was that Abigail would have exchanged all her money, her Audi car, her jewellery, and the house for a baby.

"Once round the green, and then home," Abigail told Sam, who was already panting. "And I'm keeping you on the lead, I don't want you chasing Mr and Mrs Duck."

Two figures sat on the bench, an adult and a child. They seemed familiar. Abigail had no intention of walking anywhere near them until a movement caught her eye. For the first time, she looked directly at the pair. A blackbird sang in the willow tree.

Was the woman beckoning to her? Surely not!

The old lady wore something shapeless that almost reached the floor. Her feet, encased in ancient suede brogues, sat side by side on the ground, peeping out from under the hemline of her skirt. A shawl was thrown over her head and shoulders, so only her weather-worn face and hands were visible. It was the gypsy and child Abigail had seen earlier, walking down the lane.

The child sat still. Only his hands moved, making restless shapes in his lap.

The old woman beckoned again, and Abigail glanced over her shoulder, checking that the signal wasn't intended for someone else.

"Sit for a moment," commanded the old woman.

"Me?"

"Yes. We mean you no harm. Sergei, move along and make space for the pretty lady."

"Honestly, it's quite okay..."

"You don't want to sit with us?"

Abigail didn't, but she was far too well-mannered to say so. Sergei shuffled along and regarded her steadily with small dark eyes set in a pale face. His fingers never stopped their manic dance.

Abigail sat, and Sam flopped down at her feet.

"Bufniță has been waiting for you," breathed the old woman.

4

"*P*ardon?"

Abigail caught the scent of wood smoke on the old woman's clothes. Her breath smelled of onions. She leaned in closer and Abigail tried hard not to recoil.

"You come from the big white house down the lane. The one with the long gravel drive and grounds," said the crone.

It was a statement, not a question.

"Er...yes. That's right. My name is Abigail. And you are..."

"My real name doesn't matter. I am a wise woman who has watched the years pass. They call me 'the owl' in my language, Romanian. Bufniță."

"Well, I'm very pleased to meet you, er...Bufniță," said Abigail, and turned slightly, meaning to offer her hand for shaking.

For the first time, she looked directly into the old woman's eyes. It was as though the returning, unblinking gaze was sucking her in and Abigail felt the sensation of swaying, spinning, falling. She stopped breathing.

The blackbird in the willow tree burst into song again and Abigail shivered, snapping herself out of it. She was being ridiculous!

"You said you were waiting for me?"

"*Da.*"

Abigail waited.

"*Da.* Life is made from many crossroads. We walk our paths, so smooth and flat, then suddenly, *poof!*"

The old woman's small clenched fist struck her other palm, making Abigail jump.

"Bufniță will put crossroads in your path, Abigail. Bufniță has something for you worth more than all the gold in the world. But only if you choose to take that path."

"What path? I'm sorry, I don't understand."

"You will. If you want to."

"What do you mean?"

"Bufniță has told you. She has been waiting for you. At last you are sitting beside her. Bufniță can offer you something priceless. Be warned, it won't be easy and later you may feel as though your heart is being ripped from your chest. But that will pass, and you will be happy. Bufniță can say no more until you cross her palm with gold."

"Gold? I don't have any gold! I just came out to walk the dog!"

The old woman's eyes were transfixed by the watch that flashed in the sunlight on Abigail's agitated wrist. The small boy's fingers stopped their crazy dance in his lap.

"My watch? But that's a Tiffany watch! It's worth…"

"The choice is yours."

"I can't just give you my watch! In exchange for what? None of this makes any sense and it's time I was going."

"Wait."

The old woman's claw shot out and clutched her arm. Her eyes bored into Abigail's.

"You can go, yes, and forget this day. You can go and live your empty life, and tell the time by the gold watch on your wrist. Or you can give Bufniță the watch and she will change your life. What is the time now?"

Abigail glanced at her wrist.

"Nearly a quarter past three."

"Abigail, listen to me." The old woman gripped tighter, her nails digging into Abigail's skin through her sleeve. "Give Bufniță the watch and she will give you her promise. You know the woods where we camp?"

Abigail nodded.

"Come to the woods when the sun reaches that same spot in the sky tomorrow. Come to the place where we travellers camp, by the Wishing Rock, and all will be revealed. If Bufniță does not keep her promise, you may call the police and report that Bufniță stole your watch from you. Look, the lady in the Post Office sees everything from her shop. She will have noticed that you are sitting with Bufniță and Sergei. She will back you up."

Abigail looked across the green to the Post Office in the distance. Jayne Fairweather was sorting a display outside the shop. Abigail waved, and Jayne waved back.

Abigail wasn't really the impetuous type. She liked to think about all her decisions, weigh them up, and consider them from all angles. But for some inexplicable reason, she was ready to take a risk that day.

With one smooth movement, she unclasped the watch and pressed it into Bufniță's dirty hand. Bufniță's claw closed round it. Sergei's fingers resumed their crazy dance on his lap, but his expression never changed.

"You have done well, Abigail Martin," whispered the old woman. "You have chosen the right fork of the crossroads."

Abigail was in shock.

As she walked back over the green, past the mothers collecting their children now that the school bell had rung, she shook her head. Had she really just struck up a conversation with a gypsy woman? Had she *really* handed her the Tiffany watch Aiden had given her last Christmas?

Crazy!

The remainder of the day crawled by and that night she slept fitfully, visions of Bufniță's craggy weather-worn face entering her dreams. The next day was no better, and Abigail kept catching herself checking the time.

Aiden phoned, as he did most days, although Abigail couldn't help noticing that his calls had become shorter and shorter.

Perhaps that's because he's coming home very soon, she thought, her stomach flipping with excitement at the thought.

"So, any news in the village?" he asked.

"No, not really. Just one strange thing happened when I went for a walk yesterday, but I'll save it until you come home, then I can tell you about it properly."

"Strange thing?"

"Yes, I met an old gypsy woman."

"Sorry, Abs. I have to go. I'm looking forward to hearing the whole story when I come home this weekend. Must go, love you, bye…"

Abigail leaned back in her chair, her hands around the coffee mug decorated with two intertwined *As* that Aiden had given her last Valentine's Day. It was only two-thirty, and her appointment with Bufniță was not for another half hour.

What was Abigail expecting? A box of treasure? She certainly wasn't short of money. Did she want some abstract wish granted, like happiness? Abigail wasn't normally the type to believe in the supernatural.

No, she told herself, when she met Bufniță in the woods, she'd ask for her watch back, give her some money, and that would be the end of the whole silly business.

The phone rang again. It was Daisy.

"Abigail, sorry to be a pest, but can you give me that carrot cake recipe again, please? I can't find it and I've searched everywhere."

"Oh, like the lawnmower?"

"Oh, that was embarrassing!" laughed

Daisy. "It wasn't the gypsies at all! Which reminds me, I saw them leaving this morning."

"You what?"

"The gypsies left Sixpenny Woods this morning. I saw their convoy go past my house. Simon is delighted, and I bet all the villagers..."

"Daisy, I'll find you the recipe. Something's come up. I must fly."

Abigail slammed the phone down, her hands shaking.

Gone? The gypsies had gone? She was furious with herself. How could she be so gullible?

5

"Sam! Come on! Walkies!"

Sam couldn't believe his luck. He jumped up, thrashing his tail, and together they left the house. At the gate, Abigail turned right, heading for Sixpenny Woods, and Sam's tail beat even faster.

Resisting the urge to break into a run, she marched along the track that led into the woods. Soon, the track petered out but Abigail knew exactly where she was heading. She let Sam off the lead and he trotted ahead, occasionally stopping to sniff something irresistible.

Branches swept at her face, and the canopy overhead largely blocked out the spring sunshine. Her footsteps fell silently on the rotting leaf litter. Then the trees thinned out and she was at the clearing where the gypsies camped. The ancient granite Wishing Rock stood silent.

Apart from the remains of a bonfire in the centre, with weak wisps of smoke still curling from the charcoal, there was no sign of life. She noticed a tree with the initials CD gouged out, but it didn't look freshly carved.

No vans. No vehicles. No people. No dogs. No Bufniță.

No question. The gypsies had moved on.

Abigail kicked a tree trunk in frustration.

"Bufniță! Where are you?"

No answer.

"Bufniță! You broke your promise!"

Her voice rang through the woods but there was no reply.

How could I be so stupid? Did I really hand over my expensive watch to a complete stranger? To a gypsy woman, no less? And for what?

"Come on, Sam," she said, her heart heavy. "Let's go. We'll take a walk to the police station and have a word with Stan. Report my watch stolen."

She looked around for Sam. He was a particularly obedient dog, not given to ignoring commands. He had been trained as a guide dog for the blind, but he hadn't quite made the grade.

"Sam?"

It was a rare occurrence, but this time he refused to come to her call.

"Sam! Come on!"

Silence. Nothing stirred. Abigail squeezed her eyes shut in exasperation and concentrated, listening.

Then she heard something. A noise coming from her right. Not the noise of a dog snuffling through undergrowth, but a tiny whimper, almost a mewling.

Oh no! The gypsies have abandoned a puppy!

She swung round in the direction of the tiny sniffle and spotted Sam. He was sitting quietly beside a small bush at the edge of the clearing, his tail sweeping the ground as he looked at her.

She approached the bush carefully, and peered round it.

"Sam, what have you got there?"

What she saw turned her bones to liquid and her heart nearly beat out of her chest.

"Ohhh…"

In a straw moses basket lay a baby.

Not trusting her own eyes, she squeezed them tight, then opened them again.

The baby was still there.

Abigail drew in a long breath, then crouched beside the basket. She touched the baby's rosy cheek with the back of one tentative finger. The baby fluttered its golden eyelashes but didn't wake.

The basket looked new, as did the lacy white coverlet tucked around the baby. The baby's face was clean and beautiful, flushed by sleep.

"This is it," she whispered. "This is the treasure worth more than all the gold in the world. This is the gift Bufniță promised."

Legs shaking, she sat crosslegged beside the basket, never tearing her eyes from the baby's face.

"Who are you?" she whispered. "You don't look like a gypsy baby. Did they steal you? Is your mother looking for you?"

The baby waved a tiny fist in sleep but didn't open its eyes.

Except what she'd learned from having nieces and nephews, Abigail didn't know a lot about babies. She knew this one wasn't very old. Maybe a few weeks? As her heart thudded, she knew she had to pick up the basket, with its precious, tiny occupant, and do the right thing. She had to take it to the police station.

A little distance away something caught her eye. A bag. She leaned over and grabbed it, pulling it towards herself. She fumbled with the fastenings, curious to see what it held.

Like the basket, it looked new. It was one of those cleverly designed bags that opened out into a changing mat. And it had pockets stuffed full of all manner of baby items: bottles, formula, talcum powder, nappy cream, nappies, a pacifier and a teething ring. Everything was brand new, unused.

It's almost like a baby starter pack! she thought. *I think I was meant to find the baby and keep it!*

But Abigail wasn't a bad girl, and she

wasn't stupid. She knew she couldn't keep it.

With aching heart, she slung the bag over her shoulder, then carefully lifted the moses basket with its sleeping occupant. Somewhere not too far away, she heard a car door slam and an engine start up and speed away, but her thoughts were only on the little mite asleep in the basket.

Sam followed obediently behind as she walked out of the woods and down the lane towards home. As she reached her gate, she knew she must continue past, and walk into the village and to the police station.

Stan might not be on duty. Then what? Perhaps it would be better if I just kept the baby until the morning. It'll need feeding and changing soon. I can do that.

Her heart hammered. Straight on to the village, or home?

Instead of walking past her gate and heading for the village, she turned and followed Sam who had already swung up the path to the kitchen door.

The decision was made.

A deep feeling of contentment washed

over Abigail and the gypsy's voice rang in her ears.

You have done well, Abigail Martin. You have chosen the right fork of the crossroads.

She would keep the baby.

For the moment, anyway.

Just one night wouldn't hurt.

As she turned the key in the lock, the baby stirred. The little fists flailed, and the eyes eased open for the first time.

"It's okay, baby," whispered Abigail, "we're home."

6

$\mathcal{A}$bigail locked the door behind her and placed the moses basket on the kitchen table. The baby was more agitated now, kicking at the coverlet and beginning to screw up its face and turn its head as though searching for milk.

"Are you hungry? Just hold on, little one, I'll soon sort something out for you."

Was the baby a girl or boy? She realised she didn't know.

The first priority was food, so she pulled the tin of formula out of the bag and quickly scanned the instructions. She didn't have a steriliser, but she boiled the kettle and poured boiling water into the bottle, hoping that would do the trick instead.

How much formula to make? According to the tin, it depended on the weight of the baby.

Very carefully, she lifted the baby out of the basket. It felt warm through the little stretch suit it was wearing. A wave of tenderness swept over her as she cradled it in her arms. So young, so perfect, so innocent. She walked slowly to the bathroom and stood on the scales. She knew exactly how much she weighed, and could now calculate the baby's weight. Okay, so she needed to make about 500ml of formula. She was doing well.

She placed the baby back in the basket. Using the scoop and following the instructions to the letter, she made up the feed and set it aside to cool.

Next came the nappy change, and the revelation.

Boy? Or girl?

She opened the changing mat and gently lifted the baby into the centre of it. The baby kicked and she sensed it was getting agitated. As quickly and gently as she could, she removed the little sleep-suit and nappy.

"You're a little girl!" she breathed.

First she wiped the baby clean, then fitted a new nappy around her, pressing the adhesive strips to keep it in place.

"Well, that wasn't too hard," she said and lifted the baby into her arms.

The nappy promptly fell off.

The second attempt was more successful. Next, Abigail offered her the bottle and the baby sucked enthusiastically. She held her to her shoulder and patted her back as she had done for her nieces and nephews. She was rewarded with a fat burp. An hour later, the baby was clean, fed and drifting off to sleep again. As Abigail tidied the kitchen, a contented feeling enveloped her and she realised that the cold, gnawing sensation, deep inside her, had vanished.

With the baby asleep, she made herself something to eat and relaxed, always keeping one eye on the basket. In addition to the large table and chairs, there were two easy chairs in the huge kitchen, Aiden and Abigail's favourite places to sit on cold winter days. Abigail made herself comfortable and reached for the phone. Two messages awaited her.

The first was from Daisy.

"Abigail, don't worry about the carrot cake recipe, I found it. I've made a batch so put the kettle on tomorrow morning, and I'll bring some round. Oh, and is Aiden back early? I thought I saw his car pass our house today."

The second message was a puzzle. The caller was female, with an American accent, and the message was baffling.

"Hah! So that's how you sound! I was curious."

Who on *earth* was that? Could this day get any stranger? She played it back twice more. It made no sense at all. It must be a wrong number.

She shook her head, trying to clear it. There was no time to worry about mysterious phone calls, she had to make a plan.

Bufniță meant me to find the baby, she said to herself.

There was no doubt about that. But it

didn't mean she could keep it. She couldn't keep a baby a secret, and Aiden would never allow her to keep it. No, she'd have to report it to the police.

Or did she? *What if she just packed the two of them up and left? Ran away?*

But what about the baby's mother? There may be distraught parents somewhere, desperate to find their tiny daughter.

Exhausted, Abigail fell asleep, only to be woken a few hours later by a hungry baby demanding a feed.

The bathroom door was open, framing Martha as she applied her make-up and brushed her hair.

Aiden looked at her. Had he ever really been attracted to this woman? What had he been thinking? Risking his marriage for a romp with this cold-eyed, unfeeling ice queen?

There was no question about it, she was beautiful to look at. But behind that soft skin and those wondrous curves beat a heart of granite.

"Why are you staring at me?" she asked, looking straight at Aiden. "Are you going to miss me? That's a laugh! Believe me, I won't miss you or your horrid little country. Go back to your waiting angel in Ten Cent Dump or whatever your precious village is called. Me? I'm counting the hours until I get back to New York where I do belong."

By morning, Abigail had perfected the maternal art of carrying an infant on one's hip whilst carrying out chores. She had tidied the kitchen and sorted all manner of stuff without needing to put the infant down, but she still hadn't decided what to do next.

The problem was, she didn't want to do *anything*. She wanted time to freeze and the world to leave her and her baby alone.

She jumped as somebody knocked on the kitchen door.

"Abigail? It's me! Put the kettle on."

Abigail took a deep breath and unlocked the door to let Daisy in.

"Oh my! Who is this adorable little munchkin?"

"Um, I don't actually know. It's quite a story…"

"Well! I can't wait to hear this one! What do you mean, you don't know? Is Aiden back?"

"No, I'm on my own, except for this little sweetie, of course. Aiden will be back this weekend."

"Hold on, let me make coffee and cut us some carrot cake, then you can explain."

Daisy listened carefully as Abigail told her story, only interrupting when something didn't seem clear.

"Hang on, you gave the gypsy your watch?"

"Yes, I don't know what came over me really, I just felt I had to take the risk."

She continued the story.

"And there was nobody else in the woods?"

"Nobody. I didn't see anybody. All the gypsies and their stuff had gone."

"But the baby made a sound?"

"Yes. Thank goodness I heard her, and Sam had already found her. He just sat there beside the basket, waiting for me to go over."

"And were there no clues in the bag? Or in the basket?

"None."

"Abigail, you know you can't keep her, don't you?"

Abigail cast her eyes down. She didn't answer.

"Abigail, are you listening?" Daisy's voice was gentle. "I know how much you want a baby, but this isn't the way. Imagine the despair of the parents of this little munchkin. You *have* to report this."

Abigail lifted her head and stared back at her friend with hurting eyes.

Loud banging on the front door made them both jump.

"I'll go," said Daisy.

$\mathcal{A}$bigail buried her face in the baby's neck, inhaling, breathing in the scented warmth. She heard Daisy opening the front door and talking to somebody, then she popped her head round the kitchen door.

"It's a delivery. Don't worry, I'll handle it. No need to disturb the little munchkin."

She vanished again and Abigail could hear thumping and moving noises coming from the hall. By the sounds of it, it was quite a big delivery. Perhaps Aiden had ordered something and forgotten to tell her about it?

At last the noises stopped, the front door

closed, and Daisy came back into the kitchen.

"Whew," she said, dropping an envelope onto the table beside the untouched carrot cake and heading for the sink to wash her hands. "That was a big delivery! I got them to pile it all up in the hall."

"Thank you," said Abigail, tearing the envelope open. "I wasn't expecting anything. I wonder what it is?"

She unfolded the contents and stared. The name of the company that had delivered was Baby Magic, and Abigail ran her eye down the list of items delivered.

"What…"

Daisy looked over her shoulder and read aloud.

"Baby bath, blankets, steriliser, bottles, nappies, nappy cream, a dozen tins of formula, travelling cot, clothes, more clothes, high chair, car seat, stroller… Abigail, did you order all this?"

"No! Of course I didn't!"

"Well, then who did?"

"I don't know!"

"Does the delivery note show who ordered?"

"No, it just says 'paid in full with cash' and my address."

"Do you think it's a mistake? Delivered to the wrong address?"

"Nobody has a newborn baby around here."

The two women stared at each other.

"Or was it the gypsy woman?"

"I doubt it. Why would she buy all this for me?"

"What does it say on the envelope?"

Abigail picked it up, and stared at the neat typed words on the front.

Tiffany Martin
    12, Sixpenny Lane,
    Sixpenny Cross.

Daisy saw the blood drain from her friend's face and snatched the envelope to read it for herself.

"Tiffany?"

"My watch…"

"I know. This is surreal."

Abigail clutched the baby closer to her. In that moment, she knew that if she was allowed to keep this baby, her name would be Tiffany. But her heart was full of dread. This baby would soon be taken from her. Very soon.

"Does Aiden know about any of this?"

"No, of course not. You know how he feels about adoption."

"Abigail, before this gets any deeper, I want you to phone the police station. You need to tell them everything, the whole story. You *can't* just keep this baby."

"I know."

"Do you want me to do it for you?"

A tear trickled from the corner of Abigail's eye.

"Yes. You do it."

"Right. I'll find the number."

Abigail stood up and began to pace the floor, cradling Tiffany in her arms. The baby was already asleep, but Abigail walked up and down, up and down, as Daisy dialled.

"Hello? Is that Stan? ... Hello, Stan, this is Daisy Grainger. ... Yes, I'm fine, thank you, and so is Simon. ... No, it's nothing about lawnmowers! I'm actually phoning from Abigail Martin's house in Sixpenny Lane. We have a bit of a situation here. … No, no, it's not an emergency exactly, but it is a police matter, and I think it might be a good idea if you could come round as soon as possible? … No, it's a bit delicate, I'd rather we explain when you come. … Good. We'll see you then. Goodbye, thank you."

Abigail paced up and down, up and down, her head bent low over the sleeping child.

"Well, that's good then," said Daisy brightly. "Stan is going to hop onto his bike and come round right away."

Abigail didn't reply. Instead, she began humming a tuneless song as she walked up and down, up and down.

Martha snapped her pink designer suitcase shut.

"That's it then, all packed. I'm gonna walk right out of your life. New York, here I come and it just can't come soon enough for me!"

"No hard feelings, eh?"

"Aiden, don't be an idiot. You never meant anything to me."

"Martha…"

"Come on! I don't think I ever meant much to you either. We worked together, we played together a few times, hey - we even lived together! We got that contract together, but this is where it all ends. We both gained from the arrangement, but we draw the line now."

"Will you be okay?"

"Of course! I came to England with one thing on my mind. I wanted to make me a load of bucks. And I have. We got paid handsomely for that contract, as you know, but your little, er, contribution, was the icing on the cake!"

"Will you keep in touch?"

"Nah, what for? I'm done here. I'm ready to start frying other fish."

Aiden held out his hand to touch her arm, but Martha backed away.

"So long," she said, her ridiculously high

heels clacking on the marble floor as she and her pink suitcase headed for the private lift. She pressed the button and the lift doors slid apart.

"Martha…"

"Enjoy your life in Ten Cent Dump. Enjoy your dull little wife. I'm outta here."

The lift doors whooshed shut behind her, but Aiden remained transfixed for a very long time.

8

"Come on in, Stan. Mind the boxes. Abigail's just had a rather big delivery, but we'll explain about all that. She's in the kitchen."

Stan side-stepped round one box, but managed to trip over a smaller one poking out cheekily.

When they reached the kitchen, Sam wagged his tail and Abigail looked up from her easy chair. She was still cradling Tiffany, but at the sight of the policeman, her grip tightened.

"Morning, Mrs Martin."

Abigail said nothing, but gave the police officer a half smile.

"Please sit down, Stan. I'll make us all a nice cup of tea while Abigail tells you the story."

Stan pulled out a chair and sat down. He looked from Daisy to Abigail and then to the tiny baby she held in her arms.

"It all began the day before yesterday on the village green," said Abigail dully. "And now I have Tiffany, and I don't think I can let her go."

Stan waited.

"She's very upset," said Daisy, plonking the teapot on the table. "Abigail, shall I tell the story? You can stop me if I forget anything."

Abigail nodded, her blonde head bowed over the infant.

Daisy sat down, poured tea, and started. As soon as she got to the part where Abigail handed over the watch, Stan held up his hand.

"Hold on, Mrs Grainger, I think I'll take notes as you talk, if you don't mind."

He slipped out a notebook and patted his uniform pockets, searching for a pen. He found one and began writing.

"Did the gypsy woman give you her name?"

"Bufniță," whispered Abigail. "She said it meant 'owl' in Romanian."

Stan scribbled in his notebook. The ink was refusing to flow properly but he'd be able to read the dents in the paper later.

Daisy continued, with Abigail supplying further details when asked.

"And this is the basket you found the baby in?" asked Stan, pointing with his pen.

The pen lid fell off, bounced on the floor, and rolled under the table. He bent down to pick it up, bumping his head on the table edge as he straightened up.

"Yes, that's the basket," said Abigail, ignoring the incident.

Daisy went on to describe how Abigail had brought the baby home and cared for her overnight.

"And the next thing that happened was a banging on the door. I answered it for Abigail, and it was the delivery. Well, you've seen the packages and boxes in the hall. Piles of baby stuff, all brand new. Here is the delivery note."

Stan looked at the envelope with interest.

"Tiffany? Wasn't your watch a Tiffany watch?"

Both Abigail and Daisy nodded.

"Well, this is quite a story," said Stan, closing his notebook with a decisive snap. "I think we have quite a bit to work on. I'm going to go back to the station and make a start. The gypsies won't be hard to track down, so they'll be interrogated. We also have this delivery note to check up on. Do you mind if I take it with me?"

Abigail shook her head.

"Then there's the watch. Perhaps it was offered to pawn shops recently. Also, we need to search Sixpenny Woods thoroughly, there may be clues left behind. And of course we'll check that no babies have been reported missing or kidnapped."

"And Tiffany?"

"I was coming to that. Social Services are terribly overstretched, and I was wondering whether you would be kind enough to consider looking after the baby for the moment? I can see she's very comfortable here, and this case may take a little while to sort out."

Abigail's whole demeanour changed. She sat straight in her chair, and a huge smile lit her face.

"Oh, I'd *love* to!" Abigail bent down and kissed the baby's head. "Hear that, Tiffany? You're staying for the moment."

"Brilliant!" said Daisy. "That's great news."

"Right," said Stan, getting up and making the table rock. "I'd better get the ball rolling. Mrs Martin, you will get a visit from the local Health Visitor, just to check the baby is okay. And a visit from Social Services to sign a few papers about the fostering. Of course it'll need a signature from your husband, too. Is he due back home soon?"

Had Abigail's head not been bowed over Tiffany, the policeman would have seen a flash of fear cross her face.

"Yes, Aiden is coming back tomorrow evening," said Daisy.

"Right, thank you, I'll be in touch. I'll see myself out," said Stan, going out into the hall.

The ladies heard him stumbling over the boxes in the hallway, then close the front door.

"Well, that went well!" said Daisy. "I think Stan has loads of good leads to chase up. Bet nothing so exciting has happened in Sixpenny Cross for decades! And you get to keep the munchkin for the moment."

"But what am I going to tell Aiden?" wailed Abigail. "He'll never sign any papers to foster a baby!"

"You don't know that."

"I do! You know how much I love him, but that's one thing we have *never* agreed about. We've had this conversation so many times. I've always said I'd consider adoption if we can't have children of our own. He always said he never would. He says if I don't fall pregnant, then we aren't meant to have children. He's an only child, you know.

I don't think he has the same need to have children as I do."

"Let's wait and see, shall we? You are only fostering after all. Perhaps he'll fall in love with the little munchkin, just like you did. Remember how he didn't want a dog? And then one day you brought a puppy home. Look how he loves Sam now!"

Sam heard his name mentioned and swept the floor with his tail.

Abigail said nothing. She knew that Aiden would never agree to Tiffany staying, temporarily or permanently.

The next day and a half flew past. The Health Visitor called and checked Tiffany over and pronounced her wonderfully fit and well.

"How old do you think she is?" asked Abigail.

"I'd say she's about three weeks old, and doing well. We'll keep an eye on her weight to check that she's gaining weight steadily, as she should be. I must say, you are doing a grand job! Any problems or questions I can help you with?"

"No, thank you. She's as good as gold."

"Good, I'll pop in again soon."

Abigail had begun to plunder the boxes in the hall. While Tiffany slept, she read the baby care books from cover to cover. The stroller was now assembled and, when Tiffany was fractious, Abigail pushed her around the house and garden.

"Listen, that's a blackbird singing his heart out. He's probably got a wife and babies somewhere close. And look, there's a robin redbreast. See how bold he is sitting on the fence?"

Abigail couldn't remember when she had been happier. The birdsong, the kaleidoscope of spring flowers, and the baby in the pram, all made her heart dance with joy.

It couldn't last.

Abigail stowed the tins of formula in a kitchen cupboard, and the steriliser on the counter. The baby bath was in one of the bathrooms and tiny baby clothes were folded and neatly put away in the chest of drawers in the little room next to their master bedroom. Abigail had always thought it would make a lovely nursery.

Mrs Robinson from Yewbridge County Social Services rang the bell.

"Hello, I'm Tina Robinson," she said, showing Abigail her badge. She glanced down at her clipboard. "And you must be Abigail Martin."

"Yes, that's me," smiled Abigail. "Please come in."

Mrs Robinson had a warm manner and kindly smile, but she was also a very shrewd individual. Her eyes darted everywhere, missing nothing, and she approved of what she saw. The house was clearly clean and comfortable.

Abigail led her into the kitchen where Tiffany was asleep in the moses basket.

"Here she is. I'm calling her Tiffany for the moment."

Tiffany sighed in her sleep, and the two ladies smiled.

"What a sweet thing," whispered Mrs Robinson. "It's hard to believe that any parent could abandon their baby, but sadly, sometimes it happens. We're so grateful to you for fostering this little one until we find her mother."

Abigail smiled again.

"It really is my pleasure," she said, meaning it from the depths of her being.

"The Health Visitor tells me that she's very happy for the baby to stay with you. If you could just sign here," said Mrs

Robinson, "then I'll come back early next week to get your husband's signature. Is that okay?"

A dark cloud flitted across Abigail's soul.

"Yes," she said.

It isn't 'okay' at all, screamed her heart.

Stan phoned a couple of times to keep her in the loop.

"There are absolutely no reports of any babies being kidnapped," he said. "In fact, nobody has reported a missing child in the whole country for several months."

"That's good to hear."

"We found the gypsies," Stan continued. "They moved into the next county. My colleagues gave them a visit, and found the old lady who calls herself Bufniță."

Abigail's heart lurched. She held her breath.

"The old woman refused to admit to anything except that she met you for the first time on the village green when you were walking your dog."

"That's true," said Abigail. "And Jayne Fairweather at the Post Office will tell you the same. She saw us that afternoon."

"Bufniță said she didn't know anything about your watch, denied even having noticed it. She totally denied leaving a baby in Sixpenny Woods, or knowing anything about an abandoned baby. The gypsies allowed my colleagues to search the camp and there was no sign of the watch, or anything to lead them to believe they might have had a baby in their midst recently."

Abigail felt strangely relieved.

"We haven't got very far with the delivery note, I'm afraid. The goods were paid for in cash so there's no paper trail. The shop is holding a spring sale at the moment, and they've had crowds in. They hired temporary staff for the checkouts, and nobody remembers who served that customer. Their security cameras haven't helped either."

"Did you find any clues in the woods?"

"No, nothing. Just recent signs of the gypsy encampment, as we expected. Never mind, we'll keep investigating, something will turn up."

Abigail quietly prayed that nothing would.

Aiden phoned. Uncharacteristically, she didn't pick it up, but held her breath as she listened to his message.

"Hi Abs, I expect you're out walking Sam. Sorry to have missed you, but I'll be back tomorrow anyway, so don't bother trying to catch me. The contract is all sewn up, and I can't wait to be home! I reckon I'll have packed up by the afternoon, and, allowing for traffic, I should be with you early evening. Can't wait to see you! Love you, bye."

Abigail knew she should be pleased, but she wasn't. Without any doubt, Aiden's homecoming spelled the end of her motherhood. There was no way Aiden would allow Tiffany to stay. No way that he would sign the Social Services fostering papers. And if no trace of Tiffany's parents was found, no way he'd ever agree to adopting her.

There was nothing she could do. Nothing.

Or was there?

Abigail pressed Tiffany to her chest and began to pace up and down, up and down, humming tunelessly.

Aiden's eyes flicked to the clock on the dashboard. Half past eight already. A bit later than he'd guessed but rush-hour traffic was always unpredictable, and Fridays were the worst.

His fingers raked through his dark hair, then he drummed impatiently on the steering wheel. Soon he'd pass through Yewbridge. Even though the wide roads would become twisty country lanes, he estimated he should be in Sixpenny Cross by nine o'clock.

"You usually complain that there's not enough police work to keep you busy in

Sixpenny Cross," said Sally Cooper, smiling and shaking her head.

"I know," said Stan, kissing his wife's cheek. "This case is really unusual. I thought finding the mother of this baby would be a simple matter, but I was wrong. I've got nowhere with it. And I've only just put the phone down and locked the office."

"I wonder who her parents are, poor little mite," said his wife. "Look, why don't you pop over the road for a pint to relax you? I'll have your dinner ready in about half an hour."

"Great idea, thank you. I'll be back in thirty minutes."

Through the window, Sally watched her husband walk across the road and enter the Dew Drop Inn. She put the shepherd's pie into the oven and began to lay the table.

Well, she thought, *that little baby girl was lucky to end up with Abigail Martin. Nice girl, and not short of money either, thanks to her husband's high-powered job. Just a pity it keeps him in the city so much of the time.*

It was nearly nine o'clock. Being spring, it was still light outside, although twilight was setting in. Abigail kissed Tiffany's warm head and laid her in the moses basket, tucking the coverlet round her securely. The baby lay still, with open eyes, contented after her feed.

Abigail stared out of the window and down the drive, waiting, waiting. Then she stared back at the baby.

I'm sorry, Tiffany, I think our time together has come to an end.

In the distance, up the lane, she saw headlights twinkling and a terror overcame her.

Abigail gasped.

No! No! Aiden will not make me hand Tiffany over to a complete stranger! I won't allow it!

Her heart thudded.

Crossroads time. Come on, Abigail! You have to choose right now. Aiden, or Tiffany? Choose!

10

For a split second she deliberated as the headlights approached.

Then she made her decision.

She grabbed the bottles of pre-prepared formula from the fridge, and a handful of disposable nappies.

Aiden's car swept up the drive, tyres crunching on the gravel.

Stuffing the bottles and nappies into the end of the moses basket, her head whipped round to see what else she could quickly grab. A few items of Tiffany's clothes from the clean laundry pile, the flashlight from the drawer, her jacket from the back of the chair.

Aiden climbed out of his car, opened the boot and lifted out his suitcase. He locked the car and strode up to the front door.

Abigail snatched up the moses basket and her keys. Sam jumped up and wagged his tail furiously.

"Not now, Sam," she hissed. "Lie down!"

As Aiden turned his key in the front door lock, Abigail was slipping out through the back door and into the night.

There weren't many customers in the Dew Drop that night, which pleased Stan Cooper. He'd had a heavy day, and he felt like relaxing. A nice cool glass of beer and then home to a steaming shepherd's pie. Perfect.

"Evening, Stan," said Angus, the landlord, polishing glasses and holding them up to the light. "Your usual?"

"Thanks, Angus."

"Tough day? Caught a cyclist without their lights on? Archie Draper been speeding on his tractor again?"

"Now, stop that!" said Stan, laughing.

"As it happens, I'm working on quite a puzzler at the moment."

"Can you talk about it?"

"Yes, I can give you brief details. Who knows, you may be able to shed some light on the matter. I know you hear a lot of what goes on in the village."

Angus passed the foaming beer glass to Stan and waited. He was a good listener, an essential trait for a pub landlord, and one of the reasons that the Dew Drop Inn continued to thrive.

He glanced round the bar. Nobody needed serving at the moment. His regulars, the Captain and his friend were playing dominoes in the corner by the fire, their usual spot. They were wrapped up in their game, and the group by the window were chatting, enjoying their drinks and each other's company. Idly wiping the counter with a cloth, he turned back to the policeman, ready to hear the story.

Stan took a sip from his beer and looked at Angus over his glass, not noticing the beermat still stuck to the base of the glass.

"Somebody found a baby in Sixpenny Woods this week."

"A baby? Oh no! You're joking!"

Being a pub landlord, Angus had heard his fair share of strange stories, but this surprised him.

"No, I'm not joking. Not something that happens every day in Sixpenny Cross, is it?"

"Was it a teenage mother abandoning a newborn, do you think?"

"Unlikely."

"Then it must be the gypsies."

"At the moment we don't know."

"Is the baby okay?"

"Yes, it's a little girl, about three weeks old. Beautifully dressed and looked after which rather blows the theory of an unwanted teen pregnancy."

"Must be the gypsies then."

"Except that we've interviewed them, and they insist they know nothing about any babies."

"Well, you know gypsies. And they have a reputation for stealing babies."

"We'll have to follow every lead. At the moment, nobody has reported any baby missing. So I take it that you've heard nothing here in the pub about a baby? No gossip?"

"Nope, nothing," said Angus, shaking his head, "but I'll certainly be listening out from now on."

***

"Abigail! I'm home!"

The house was silent, apart from Sam who bounded up to Aiden, tail wagging furiously in welcome. Aiden patted him on the head then called his wife again.

"Abs?"

No reply.

Aiden dumped his suitcase beside the boxes in the hall and went into the kitchen. The light was on, and the back door was unlocked, but there was nobody there.

He walked from room to room, calling Abigail, finishing his search in the bedroom. Everywhere were signs of a baby in residence. Aiden's face was white and bloodless. He opened their phone book, searching for a number.

"Daisy, is Abigail with you? I've just got home and there's no sign of her."

"Oh, hi Aiden! Glad you're home. No, Abigail isn't with me. Is her car in the drive?"

"Yes, it's parked as usual."

"Perhaps she's taken Sam out for a quick walk?"

"No, Sam's here with me. Daisy, everywhere I look in the house, I see baby stuff. What on *earth* is going on?"

A long pause.

"She hasn't told you anything?"

"No."

Another long pause.

"Well, Aiden, it's not my place to tell you really. I think you need to discuss it with Abigail."

"But she's not here!"

"If you are really worried, perhaps you should talk to Stan."

"Stan Cooper? The policeman?"

"Yes."

"Thank you, Daisy, I'll consider that."

With a shaking hand, Aiden replaced the receiver, then searched the house again, calling Abigail as he went. He opened the back door and turned on the outside garden lights. Nothing moved. No sounds apart from an owl calling in Sixpenny Woods.

"Abs! Are you out here?"

No response.

Aiden went back inside and wondered what to do. He sat at the kitchen table and put his head in his hands.

In the little guest cottage in the garden, Abigail crouched in the dark, listening. She'd heard Aiden open the back door. She'd moved away from the window when he flooded the garden with light. When he called her, she shuddered and shrank down. She'd prayed that Tiffany wouldn't make a sound, and she hadn't.

The guest cottage was comfortable, with everything provided that a guest might need. It had a kitchen, a living room, bedroom and bathroom. It was brand new, rarely used. It was a perfect hide-out, but not for long. She couldn't stay there, she'd soon be discovered.

What to do? Ideally, she'd get to her car and drive away. The problem was that Aiden would hear her feet crunching across the gravel. She'd have to wait here in the guest cottage until the coast was clear, then get to her car. But she couldn't do that unless Aiden went out or went to bed. And if she did manage to get to the car, then what? Where would she drive to?

Daisy's? No, Daisy was too sensible. She wouldn't approve of what Abigail was doing. She'd make her go back to Aiden, and then there'd be fireworks. Aiden would say they couldn't keep Tiffany, and Tiffany would be taken away. No, she couldn't go to Daisy.

Perhaps her sister in Yewbridge? Abigail considered that one. It was a possibility.

Abigail's thinking was muddled. Distress was eating away at her and she'd lost the ability to make rational decisions. She was mentally exhausted, and her mind was jumbled. Only one idea remained clear in her head: every moment she had with Tiffany was precious. She needed to watch and wait until the lights went off and the coast was clear. She began humming softly.

Inside the main house, Aiden was still in

the kitchen, fretting. Should he follow Daisy's advice and phone the police? Or wait? Perhaps Abigail would walk through that door any moment.

But he knew she wouldn't. In spite of the lateness of the hour, he reached for the phone.

11

Flying was not an activity Martha Guttman particularly enjoyed, although Business Class seats did make the experience somewhat less gruelling. Sitting still for long periods of time was not something she found easy.

None of the movies offered interested her and she'd already had a manicure and hand massage. Now she was thirsty. Irritably, she pressed the button to summon the hostess.

In the galley, the two air hostesses on duty exchanged glances when Martha's seat number buzzed and lit up.

"Your turn," said one. "I waited on her ladyship last time."

The other nodded, smoothed her hair and made her way down the aisle to Martha's seat. She drew the curtain aside a fraction and popped her head round, smiling.

"You rang?"

"Tea. Earl Grey. In a proper china cup and saucer."

"Yes, ma'am."

If the curtain hadn't swung back, Martha would have seen the hostess make a face and roll her eyes.

Martha stretched her feet, hoping the flight wasn't going to make her ankles swell. Earlier she had raised her leg and stretched her toes and noticed the man across the aisle gawking at her. That's why she'd drawn the curtain.

Men! Gee, they were so stupid. And so easy to control. She'd been shipped over from the New York office specifically to work on this contract with Aiden. And Aiden was cute, but stupid. A perfect short-term distraction.

Reeling in Aiden like a fish had been child's play. All she had to do was smile at him, and laugh at his stupid jokes. Of course the short skirts had helped, and the way she sat just a little too close when they worked on papers together.

Huh! What's a girl supposed to do to entertain herself when she's so far from home? She was bored, and Aiden was available.

The company, keen to impress the clients, provided them with a penthouse suite in the heart of the city. It served as an office as well as somewhere to conduct important conferences. It also had two separate bedrooms, one of which was abandoned a few times when her strategy to seduce him succeeded. His initial protests about his silly little wife in Ten Cent Dump had been easily brushed aside.

It was all temporary, anyway. Martha didn't want to stay in the UK, she missed the razzle-dazzle and energy of New York City.

It had taken a year of hard work, but they'd won the contract which had earned them both a great deal of money in bonuses.

If only she hadn't made that one stupid mistake…

But even that had turned out hunky-dory in the end.

Hadn't it?

Better than okay. Gee, Aiden had handed her *even more* dollars to keep her quiet. She smiled as she thought of her extremely healthy bank balance.

Yep, she'd done the right thing accepting it.

Hadn't she?

Tufty, the Cooper's scruffy brown and white dog, jumped up excitedly and wagged his stumpy tail in welcome.

"Ah, you're back, good timing," said Sally Cooper to her husband.

She opened the oven door and slid the piping hot shepherd's pie out. It was golden brown and slightly crispy on the top. Perfect.

"Dinner's ready. Did you enjoy yourself? Relax a bit?"

"Thanks, yes," said Stan as he washed his hands and splashed water on Sally's clean floor. "I had a good chat with Angus behind the bar, but unfortunately, he hasn't heard anything. My, that pie smells good."

Before he had the chance to sit down, the phone rang. Stan and Sally looked at each other. Phone calls at that time of night were not good news. It usually meant that the call had been diverted from the police station next door, and something needed urgent attention.

"I'll get it," said Stan heavily, and lifted the receiver. "PC Cooper here, how can I help you?"

"Ah, Stan, it's Aiden Martin here, Abigail Martin's husband."

"Good evening, sir."

He waited. Often people needed a moment to collect themselves before speaking to the police.

"Stan, I've just got back from London expecting Abigail to be here, but there's no sign of her. The house is empty, except for baby stuff. I phoned Daisy Grainger and she doesn't know where my wife is, and she wouldn't tell me anything. She told me to get the story from you."

"Right, sir."

Stan looked at the shepherd's pie waiting for him, then at Sally poised with the serving spoon.

"Do you think you could wait half an hour? The thing is, I haven't eaten yet. I'll just have a quick bite then I'll cycle up to you. If Mrs Martin turns up in the next half hour, give me a call."

He nodded at Sally, and the serving spoon descended, digging into the pie. Stan's mouth watered.

"Yes, that's fine," said Aiden trying hard not to sound worried. "Thank you. I'll leave the lights on in the drive and I'll see you soon."

From the dark of the guest cottage in the back garden, Abigail could clearly see Aiden in the lit kitchen of the house. She saw him talking on the phone. Then she saw him put his head in his hands again.

For a moment she was tempted to go to him. She pictured herself entering the kitchen and putting her arms round him, telling him not to worry. But one glance at the sleeping baby in the basket stopped her. Aiden wouldn't understand.

At the first opportunity, she'd get to her car and escape.

She hummed tunelessly under her breath and waited.

In the Cooper household, Stan was mopping his plate clean with a slice of bread.

"Delicious," he said. "The last thing I feel like doing is cycling up to the Martin's house now, but I think I must. Strange that Mrs Martin is missing. I imagine there's a simple reason for it."

"I think it's very strange that Mr Martin didn't know anything about the baby," Sally remarked.

Stan reluctantly climbed on his bike and cycled through the village and up the lane to the Martin's house, turning into their gravelled drive. He dismounted, and walked his bike to the front door, leaning it against the wall. He pressed the bell.

In the guest cottage, Abigail had stopped humming. She stood motionless, listening. Was that somebody crunching on the gravel of their drive? When the doorbell rang in the distance, she jumped. Who could be visiting at this time of the night? From the shadows of the cottage, she watched the illuminated kitchen.

She saw Aiden stand and go to answer the door. Moments later, he returned with Stan and they both sat at the table. Abigail's jaw dropped with horror. *Aiden had called the police?*

This changed everything. How long before they searched the garden and guest cottage? And they'd hear her on the gravel if she tried to reach her car.

Reason abandoned her completely. Now she saw herself as rescuing Tiffany, and it never occurred to her that she herself might be charged with kidnapping a child.

"Sleep, little baby," she whispered. "We have to move, otherwise they'll get you."

Tucking the coverlet more tightly around

the baby, she slipped on her jacket. Lifting the moses basket by the handles, she opened the cottage door and crept outside into the garden. Aiden and Stan were still sitting at the kitchen table, deep in conversation.

The basket was heavy and cumbersome, but Abigail scarcely noticed. Avoiding the rectangle of light thrown out by the kitchen window, she skirted the garden, hugging the boundary, heading for the end.

Luckily she was very familiar with the layout, and didn't need the flashlight. She had no real plan, just a desperate desire to escape from her husband and the police.

The grounds of the house were extensive, and it took her some time to reach the spot that she had in mind. There was a break in the hedge where deer had pushed through, and Abigail planned to use it to her advantage. Now, out of sight of the house, she clicked on the flashlight and ran the beam along the hedge, searching for the gap.

There it was!

Walking backwards to protect the baby

from branches that might spring back, she pushed through and into Archie Draper's field on the other side.

Now where?

Sixpenny Woods?

She shuddered. No, too dark and full of unknown dangers. One of Archie's outbuildings would be preferable for the moment. Then, in the morning, she could keep an eye on the lane, and quickly return to collect her car if Aiden went out.

But she had to hurry. Tiffany would soon be awake for her next feed.

Archie's recently ploughed field made the ground soft under her feet. The moon wasn't full, and clouds scudded across it frequently, but there was enough light to see the big open field, and the silhouette of the farmhouse beyond it. Clustered around the farmyard were barns and outbuildings.

Abigail set off. Walking straight was easy because all she needed to do was follow the line of the furrow. Luckily there hadn't been much rain recently or the field would have been a quagmire. But it was a big field, and the basket was getting heavier and heavier. Her arms ached.

The flashlight beam began to dim, so she turned it off to conserve the battery. She could manage without it because her feet had grown accustomed to following the line of the turned earth.

She switched the basket from one hand to the other, trying to relieve her aching arms and wrists. A deer barked in the distance. Something scuttled over her shoe, but she ignored it, concentrating only on putting one foot in front of the other.

She longed to find shelter and a place to set the basket down and rest her weary limbs. Head down, she trudged on, only allowing herself the occasional glance up to see if the Drapers' farm was getting any closer.

She was sweating from exertion, the perspiration running down her face and body. She stopped, unzipped her jacket and laid it carefully over Tiffany, shielding her from the cold night air. The breeze had strengthened, and she felt both hot and cold as the perspiration sprang from her pores to be cooled immediately by the wind.

At last, when she thought her arms and legs could go no further, she reached the gate to the farmyard. Resting for a moment, she put the basket down and leaned on the gate, gathering her strength. Something rustled in the hedge beside her, but she was too tired to take fright.

No lights blazed in the farmhouse. Perhaps the Drapers were out? No. Farmers were early risers and it was more likely they had already retired to bed.

Abigail switched on the flashlight and pushed the gate open, wincing when it creaked. From inside the house, a dog barked. Abigail killed the flashlight, grabbed the basket and shrank back into the shadows.

"Tyson! Pipe down! Whatever is the matter with you?" a muffled voice shouted from inside the farmhouse.

The dog quietened down, and all was still again. The moon cast a cold pale light over bushes and buildings, creating deep shadows. Nothing stirred.

Abigail was shivering now, partly from fright and partly from the cold that had penetrated her bones now that she'd stopped walking. She slipped through the open gate and shone her torch at the first outbuilding. She tried the door, but it was locked. So was the second. She pushed the third door hard. It opened.

Hallelujah!

Inside the building, she looked around and saw bales of straw piled up to the ceiling.

We'll be warm in here for a while, she thought.

And then she had a small stroke of good fortune.

12

To Abigail's delight, the beam of her dying flashlight caught a light switch.

"Tiffany, I'm going to give you your bottle first, because I don't need light for that. By then the Drapers should be fast asleep and I can turn on the light and make us a warm, cosy den for the night."

Tiffany whimpered. It was getting close to her feed time. The fresh night air had given her an appetite and she was making it clear she was hungry. Abigail plucked her from the basket and sat on a straw bale, cuddling her close and enjoying the warmth.

She offered her the bottle and the baby sucked greedily.

Abigail's teeth were chattering. She was cold and still a little shaky from the trek, but the shelter from the wind and the baby's natural warmth were taking the chill from her bones.

The building had no windows but Abigail didn't need light for this job, it was already second nature. She never tired of giving Tiffany the bottle. Normally she watched the baby's eyelashes flutter as she fed but tonight it was too dark to see. She loved the closeness, and the little contented grunting noises Tiffany made as she sucked. Abigail hoped that it didn't matter that she hadn't warmed the bottle.

"Slow down, Tiff, you'll choke! There isn't any hurry, you know," she whispered.

No sound came from the farmhouse and even the dog was quiet.

When the baby had drunk her fill, Abigail stuffed the gap under the door with loose straw, partly to block out draughts, and partly to stop any light seeping out under the door. She switched on the light, delighted when the single dirty bulb illuminated.

She still felt cold, and her head ached, but this place would do nicely for the night.

"There we are, Tiff!" she said softly. "We're going to be fine tonight. I'm going to change your nappy, then we'll have a little play, then settle down and go to sleep."

Half an hour later, Tiffany was tucked up in her basket and dozing off. Abigail switched off the light. The straw bales served as a mattress and she curled up round the basket using her jacket as a cover. Her throat was sore and every bone ached. She desperately wanted a drink and something to eat. Eventually, she dropped into a dreamless, exhausted sleep.

As the orange morning sun rose in the chilly dawn sky, Archie Draper pulled on his wellington boots and whistled to his dog. It was his favourite time of day. Just a few chores to do before he went back inside to tuck into the breakfast Molly was making for him.

"Hey, Tyson, did I leave the gate open last night? That's not like me, must be getting old."

Tyson, nose to the ground, was busy. There were strange new scents here that needed investigating. For once he ignored the barn cats and concentrated on gathering information.

Strange humans had passed here during the night.

In the hay store, Abigail opened her eyes a crack, and listened. She felt terrible; cold, shaky and lightheaded. Every muscle ached. Her throat was sore and a desire to cough overwhelmed her. She buried her face in her jacket to muffle the inevitable sound.

"Tyson, did you hear that? Thought I heard a cough."

Abigail froze, but another cough erupted. Tyson was already barking and pawing at the door.

"Tyson, who's in there?"

Tiffany woke and began to whimper.

Abigail sat up, grabbed the handles of the basket and took a deep breath.

Archie held Tyson's collar and pushed the door open, allowing the morning light to flood into the dark interior. Disturbed dust particles danced crazily, suspended in the light. Archie Draper gaped at the scene before him. A woman and a baby in his hay store?

"What the…"

Abigail tried to stand, but the effort was too much. She sat down heavily again. At that moment, Tiffany decided that she was ravenous and began to yell. Tyson barked excitedly.

"Ye gods and little fishes! Tyson, quiet! Abigail Martin, is that you? What on earth are you doing in here?"

Abigail stared at him, then shielded her mouth as another cough racked her.

"Here, come with me, I'll take you inside. That's a nasty cough you have there. I reckon the dust from the straw has got into your throat, or you've caught a chill. Have you been here all night? The wife'll get you some hot tea and a spot of breakfast.

That'll make you feel better. Then you can tell us the whole story."

Tears trickled down Abigail's pale cheeks.

"No need to get upset!" said Archie, alarmed. "I'll take the basket, you hold the baby and hang onto my arm. You'll feel a lot better when we're inside."

Abigail allowed herself to be steered out of the store room and across the farmyard to the kitchen. Tiffany grumbled, but her yells had subsided. Archie kept up his cheery chatter, and Tyson followed, his tail wagging.

"Our kitchen is nice and warm, and I know my wife will be cracking open some new-laid eggs, and setting the table for breakfast."

Abigail didn't say a word, grateful that he didn't seem to expect a reply from her.

"Emily, put the kettle on, we've got visitors!"

His wife opened the door and her eyes widened.

"Mercy me! Come in, come in!"

"Tyson found them in the hay store,"

said Archie, as though Abigail was deaf. "She's freezing. I reckon she's caught a chill. Young 'un seems fine though."

As if to demonstrate there was nothing wrong with her, Tiffany exercised her lungs at full volume.

"Oh, my!" laughed Emily, peering at the baby's red, screwed up face. "Reckon I'll concentrate on your breakfast first, shall I? This bottle here ready to be warmed is it?"

Abigail nodded, and the farmer's wife stood the bottle in a bowl of hot water.

"Sit yourself down, my love. Take the weight off your feet. I'll have this bottle ready for this young madam or sir in two shakes of a lamb's tail. Then, when you've got some breakfast and a hot cup of tea or two down you, you can tell us all about it."

About a mile away, the climbing sun was shining down on other early risers. Stan dismounted from his bicycle and pushed it the remaining yards up the gravelled drive to the Martins' front door. He attempted to lean it against the wall, but the handlebars twisted round and it fell. His second attempt was more successful.

"Morning, sir," he said as Aiden swung the door open. "Ready to start the search now that it's light?"

"Morning, Stan, I'm more than ready. And I've just made a bit of a discovery. Somebody has been in the guest cottage. It's unlocked and the door was open a crack."

"Did you search it?"

"Yes, I think she was there, but she's gone now."

"Well, bearing in mind that Mrs Martin didn't take her car, or any possessions really, I don't believe she's gone far. Of course she was weighed down with the baby, too. And I think you would have passed her down the lane last night if she had gone that way. We know she'd only just left before you arrived because you said the water was still hot in the kettle."

"Where is she then?"

"We'll find her, sir. My intention is that we search until midday. After that, well, then we have a bit of a problem. We can't register Mrs Martin as a missing person. She's an adult and can do as she pleases. However, she's taken the baby. Unfortunately, if we go official, then she could be charged with kidnapping."

Aiden sighed. He blamed himself. Abigail had taken flight because of him. He was totally responsible. He'd made no attempt to understand how much she yearned for a baby. No, he'd not only high-handedly announced that he'd never adopt somebody else's child, but he'd also had an affair behind her back. He didn't deserve her.

No wonder she couldn't face him with a baby in her arms. No wonder she'd run away. And because of him she could now be looking at a serious criminal charge.

Aiden had lain awake most of the night, listening out for the slightest sound. His thoughts churned in his head like the contents of a cement mixer. Eventually he'd fallen into a fitful sleep, promising himself that when he found her, he'd beg her forgiveness.

"I'm guessing she didn't cross the gravel

at all, or you'd have heard her," remarked the policeman.

"What? You think she may have gone down the garden and across the fields?"

"It's possible…"

"Right! Let's go! No, Sam, you can't come."

Sam's ears were pricked and his delight at an unexpected early morning walk was evident.

"Excuse me, sir, but I think Sam might be able to help us here. He's a retriever, right?"

"Yes."

"Well, perhaps if you let him sniff something of the baby's, he might be able to help with the search?"

"Genius! Yes! Do you know, Stan, I think you may be onto something there!"

Aiden grabbed a towelling bib that was lying on the kitchen table and held it up to Sam's nose. Sam wagged his tail.

"Go find it, Sam, go find it!"

13

Sam was in his element. This is what he was born for! Feathery tail swishing furiously, he bounded out of the kitchen door and into the garden. Nose down, he trotted along the path until he came to the guest house.

The two men looked at each other. Neither man was surprised, but they were definitely impressed by the dog's sense of smell.

Aiden let Sam into the guest cottage. Sam sniffed around, particularly near the window, then ran outside again, along the hedge, towards the bottom of the garden.

"Hold on, boy," panted Aiden, and

clipped a lead onto his collar. "Okay, go find it!"

Sam usually walked perfectly on the lead, but today he was on a mission. Today he was hunting down the little human that smelled of milk. His nose never stopped working and he strained on his lead, pulling so hard that Aiden was forced to jog, the policeman trotting close behind.

Sam skirted the garden, paws soaked by the dewy grass. He followed his nose, and that took him along the hedgerow, exactly where Abigail had walked the night before. When he came to the gap in the hedge, he didn't hesitate. He pushed through, tugging his master behind him.

"Shucks!" said Stan to himself as a branch whipped back and struck his face.

Once in the field, Sam swung his head left and right, until he picked up the scent again, clear and strong.

"Looks like we're going for a trek across the field!" Stan panted.

Aiden felt a little more positive now they had a definite purpose, but he was tortured by the thought of Abigail stumbling across the field in the dead of night, clutching a newborn baby. They *must* find her. And quickly.

Abigail stared hungrily at the plate of food that Emily placed in front of her.

"There you are, my love. Two fresh, lightly boiled eggs, some buttered toast and as many cuppas as you can drink. Everything always looks better after a decent breakfast, you mark my words."

Abigail looked from Emily to the plate in front of her. She still hadn't said a word since she'd been discovered.

"Pass me that little angel," said Emily, "and I'll feed her while you tuck in. Oh my, Archie, were our kids ever this small?"

Silently, Abigail released her hold on Tiffany and watched as the baby sucked furiously on the bottle the farmer's wife offered her. Only then did she nibble on the corner of a slice of toast.

It tasted good. No, it tasted delicious. Abigail polished off both eggs, all the toast and a big mug of tea. For the first time in hours she felt warm, inside and out. Her throat was no longer sore and her headache had departed.

"You look better already," remarked Archie. "You've got some colour back in your cheeks."

"Thank you," said Abigail softly. "I'll never forget your kindness."

She looked round the comfortable, shabby kitchen and thought of her own chic one, knowing she infinitely preferred the Drapers'.

None of the chairs matched, neither did the worn, handmade cushions. In Abigail's kitchen, every chair matched, and the cushion fabric repeated the pattern on the curtains. Crockery occupied every space on the Drapers' dresser, along with a basket of eggs, and some jam jars. At home, crockery was arranged artistically on Abigail's dresser, and rarely used. Here, Tyson lay on a threadbare rug near the cooking range, compared with Sam's elegant rarely-used dog bed at home.

The kitchen table was huge, but dented

and scratched, the wood pale from decades of scrubbing. An enormous teapot dressed in a knitted tea-cosy sat in the centre.

"Another cup of tea?" asked Archie, watching her.

"Thank you, yes, I'd love one. And I owe you both an explanation."

"When you're ready, my love, no rush," said Emily.

Nobody noticed Tyson's ears prick up. Nobody saw him jump to his feet, alert, listening.

"I'm ready now," said Abigail, and took a deep breath. "You must be wondering why…"

But she never finished her sentence, because somebody knocked on the kitchen door at the same time as Tyson began barking.

Abigail leapt up, nearly knocking over her chair, and snatched Tiffany from Emily's arms.

"Don't let them take her!" she hissed, terror in her eyes.

"Nobody is going to take your baby from you," said Emily, putting her arm round her frightened guest. "Archie, open that door!"

"Stand back," he said, grabbing the poker.

He opened the door decisively, then gaped.

"Morning, Mr Draper," said Stan. "Sorry to disturb you so early. May I come in for a chat?"

Sam was already in the kitchen, renewing his acquaintance with his old friend Tyson, and greeting Abigail with delight.

"Of course," said Archie and stood back to allow the policeman entry.

"I don't think you'll be needing that!" said Stan, pointing at the poker in Archie's hand.

The intense atmosphere lightened immediately as everyone but Abigail smiled and Archie replaced the poker.

"Is Aiden with you?" she asked, white-faced.

"Yes, he's outside. I wanted to see you first."

"How did you know where I was?"

"Ah, Sam helped us there. Excellent retriever he is! Led us a merry chase through your hedge and across the fields."

Abigail forced herself to blurt out the one question that she really didn't want answered.

"Have you found out anything more about Tiffany's parents?"

"Yes."

Abigail's heart beat like a drum.

"I think the mystery has been largely cleared. We now know the identity of the baby's mother, and the father, and how you came to find her in Sixpenny Woods."

Archie and his wife exchanged glances. None of this made any sense at all.

Abigail's distress was palpable. Her knees were shaking and she sank down onto a chair, tears coursing down her face. Her hold on the baby was vice-like.

"So you are going to take Tiffany away?"

"No," said Stan gently. "No, I'm not."

"It's a trick! You're going to take her! If you *know* who the parents are, then why am I allowed to keep her? Aiden put you up to this!"

Emily rested a supportive hand on Abigail's arm.

"I'm sure that's not the case, my love," she said gently.

"It is! It is the case! Aiden will never let me foster or adopt a baby! That's why I ran away!"

Before anyone could answer, another figure stepped into the doorway. Aiden stood framed, his face strained and as pale as the milk in the chipped jug. The room fell silent.

"Abigail, Stan is telling the truth. The reason why nobody will ever take the baby away is because Tiffany is my daughter."

14

"*Right*," said Stan, breaking the silence. "I'm going to return to the station and collect my car. Then I'll come straight back and take the three of you home."

"I've chores to do outside," said Archie tactfully. "It's time I got the tractor out, those fields won't plough themselves."

He hurried out of the door, grabbing his coat and boots on the way.

"I'm going to check the ewes and collect the eggs," said Emily, zipping up her jacket and pulling on fingerless knitted gloves. "Help yourself to tea or anything you want."

It was unlikely that either Aiden or

Abigail heard her kind words or saw her leave the kitchen, they were still staring at each other, speechless.

Aiden sat down heavily.

"Abs, I'm so sorry..."

Abigail stared back at her husband with ice-cold eyes but her hold on the baby didn't loosen. She felt as if a claw had grabbed hold of her heart. She suddenly recalled the old gypsy's words.

Be warned ... you may feel as though your heart is being ripped from your chest.

Eventually she managed to force out some words. Her tone was flat, expressionless.

"I don't understand."

"Abs, everything is my fault, and I've behaved appallingly. If you never forgive me, I wouldn't blame you."

"I don't understand. Explain."

"You know how I've been working flat out on the contract... I've been away from you and Sixpenny Cross so much. I know that's no excuse, but I kind of lost my way."

"Explain." Abigail's eyes were narrow and flinty.

"I'm so sorry, Abs. I had an affair."

"Go on."

Aiden was gabbling now, eager for her to understand but mortified at having to confess.

"I had to work really closely with a woman called Martha Guttman, and we just kind of began a relationship."

Abigail snorted.

"Martha is American. We had a relationship, well, just a brief fling really. I don't think we ever had any strong feelings for each other. It didn't last long."

"How could you!" Abigail spat. "Didn't she know you were married?"

"Yes, but she didn't care."

"Neither did you, it seems."

"Abs, I'm so sorry, so very sorry. It should never have happened."

"No, you bet it shouldn't."

"And then," Aiden took a big breath, "then Martha announced she was pregnant. It was a big shock, to both of us, especially as we weren't even romantically involved. She was horrified and insisted on having an abortion, but I couldn't bear the thought of that. I persuaded her to have the baby, and then sign it over to me. She didn't take that much persuading as Martha's main interest in the world is money. So I offered her a lot, and she agreed to the deal."

Abigail simply couldn't believe what she was hearing. Had the world gone crazy?

"She gave her daughter away for *money*?"

"Yes, Martha is like that. She doesn't have a maternal bone in her body. She hated being pregnant, but she looked on it as a lucrative nine-month job. And she hated England, couldn't wait to get away when the baby was born and our work was over."

"I still don't understand. What were you planning to do with the baby?"

"At first I thought I'd just tell the truth and bring the baby home to you."

"That would have been the right thing to do."

"Yes, but I couldn't face telling you I'd had an affair. I was so ashamed." Aiden buried his face in his hands. "And so I hatched a plan. One weekend when I was home, I took Sam for a walk in Sixpenny Woods and visited the travellers. I introduced myself to Bufniţă and I told her to get you into conversation and persuade you to come to Sixpenny Woods at an appointed time. I told her that you were very kind-hearted and gullible, and that you'd probably give her your watch if she asked for it, in exchange for information."

"It was you! You set Bufniţă up! You told her to ask for my watch?"

"Yes. If you hadn't given it, she'd still have told you to go to the woods at an appointed time. I had already given her a lot of money and promised her more if you didn't give her your watch. I just thought you'd be more likely to turn up if she'd taken your watch."

"Did she know about the baby?"

"No, nothing. I just told her to get the gypsies to move on as soon as she'd got you to agree to go to the woods the next day. I needed the coast clear so I could leave the baby there for you to find."

"How *could* you! What if I hadn't come to the woods? What if somebody else found her? What if animals attacked her?"

"I was there watching all the time. You

didn't see me. I was worried that Sam would see me though."

Abigail remembered the sound of a car driving away at the time. And hadn't Daisy said that she thought she'd seen Aiden's car?

"And the delivery? I suppose you ordered all that baby stuff?"

"Yes."

"You disgust me."

"Abs. I'm sorry."

"You had an affair. You lied. You cheated. You schemed and manipulated."

"Yes."

"I don't think I can ever forgive you for this."

"Abs..."

"You betrayed me."

"Abs..."

"You tricked me into falling in love with your baby."

"Abs, she could be *our* baby if you'd only forgive me," he begged. "I'll do anything, go to counselling, anything. My brief affair with Martha made me realise how much I love you. What a fool I've been!"

"I can hardly bear to look at you."

"Abs…"

Aiden's eyes beseeched her and his hand snaked out across the table to reach hers.

"Don't touch me! I told you, I can't even bear to look at you."

Abigail looked down at the baby and stroked her soft cheek with one finger. Her mind was in turmoil. She began humming a tuneless song.

Martha paid for the postcard and walked out of the store. Central Park wasn't particularly busy, and she headed for an empty bench, her high heels and the sway in her walk attracting the attention of several men in the vicinity.

She pulled the lid off her pen, thought for a moment, then wrote a sentence. Then she wrote the destination address on the other side. She had no trouble remembering it.

12, Sixpenny Lane,

Sixpenny Cross,
Near Yewbridge,
Dorset.

Gee, what a darned stupid address!

A sparrow hopped a few feet away, searching for fallen crumbs from picnickers' packed lunches. Two fledgelings hopped behind her, beaks agape in hope. A pair of joggers ran by, then two young mothers, deep in conversation, pushing strollers. She watched them until they were out of sight.

She read her message again, nodded with satisfaction, then slipped the postcard into the nearest mailbox.

15

Stan wrapped his hands round the mug of tea his wife had handed him. Last night, when Aiden Martin had admitted to his affair and to being the father of the baby, Stan had been very surprised.

"Good gracious! Well, that's not what I expected!" Sally had said, just as surprised as her husband.

Stan had just returned from delivering Aiden, Abigail, and the baby back to their house in the lane.

"So what happened when you drove them back to their house?" Sally Cooper wanted to know now.

"They were hardly speaking. Mrs Martin

looked as though she was in shock. And Mr Martin just stared out of the window. When they got out of the car, they were very polite, but you could have cut the atmosphere with a knife."

"Who was carrying the baby?"

"She was."

"Good. She hasn't turned against the little mite then. Babies have a way of bringing people together. I guess we'll just have to wait and see."

Several days had slipped by since Aiden's revelation. In spite of what he'd done, it was hard for Abigail to simply stop loving her husband. True, he'd lost her trust, and she was still furious, but Aiden was her husband. She knew him well enough to know that he was genuinely distraught and desperately sorry for what he'd done.

In his favour, he was gentle and attentive to her at all times, and clearly adored Tiffany.

Perhaps time would heal her hurt.

Aiden came into the room.

"Good news! I've just been talking on the phone to the company. They're still thrilled about the contract being secured. I suggested that in future, I work more from home, and only go up to London for meetings. My boss was quite happy with that idea."

Abigail looked at him.

"That means I'll be home much more. I can help you, and be with you and Tiffany. Only if you'd like that, of course."

Abigail paused before speaking.

"Yes, I think I'd like that," she said at last.

Aiden stooped to drop a kiss on his daughter's head and, with a new spring in his step, headed back to the room he had converted into an office.

On the front doormat, something brightly coloured caught his eye. He picked up a postcard and stared at the picture before turning it over to read. It was a New York city skyline, instantly recognisable by the Empire State building and Twin Towers. His heart lurched. He knew only one person in New York. Turning it over, he read the message.

I'm beginning to have second thoughts about giving up the brat.

Oh no! What did it mean? Was Martha going to become a nuisance? She'd made it very clear that she didn't want to be saddled with a baby and he'd paid her handsomely. What was she playing at?

What to do?

Nothing, he decided. Except to phone the telephone company to get her calls blocked, just in case. Perhaps this was just another of Martha's malicious games.

Time is a great healer, and slowly, slowly, as the days passed, Abigail's broken heart began to mend itself. She brooded about Aiden's betrayal a little less each day and her time was taken up with the joy of raising Tiffany.

Together, she and Aiden set up Tiffany's

nursery and established a routine. Any outsider might have thought they were the perfect little family.

Aiden dared to hope that one day, Abigail would forgive him.

The only fly in the ointment was Martha. The woman was so spiteful and unpredictable. Every day he listened for the postman's footsteps on the gravel drive and made sure he was the first to pick up the mail.

The next postcard showed the Statue of Liberty against a clear blue cloudless sky. Little boats dotted the island around it. The message was terse.

Blocking phone calls from me won't work because I know where you live.

Aiden's heart went cold. Could she take Tiffany back? Or was this just another ploy for more money? Should he tell Abigail?

No, he decided, it would destroy her.

Weeks passed and things were going well between them. No more postcards arrived and Abigail seemed to be warming to him a little more each day. Next week was her birthday and he had made big plans to surprise her.

On the morning of her birthday, a timid tap on the bedroom door woke Abigail.

"Come in..."

"Happy birthday, Abs."

"You remembered."

"Of course."

Aiden came in, carrying a beautifully arranged breakfast tray complete with a tiny vase of primroses.

Abigail sat up sleepily.

"Gosh, that looks wonderful! Thank you."

"And I have something for you."

He reached into his pocket and pulled out a tiny gift-wrapped box and placed it on the tray.

"What's this?"

"Open it."

Abigail tore off the paper and opened the box. It was an exquisite Tiffany eternity ring. She gasped and looked at Aiden.

"It's beautiful."

"I had it engraved, although the writing

is so tiny you may need a magnifying glass to read it. It says 'You are my world - A'. I want you to know how sorry I am and that I will love you and Tiffany forever. I want you to think of that whenever you see the ring."

"That was a lovely thought," she said, slipping it on her finger with her engagement ring and wedding band.

Aiden smiled down at his wife. She smiled back.

"Now go and get another plate," she said. "Help me eat this lovely breakfast. There's far too much for one, and hurry up because Tiff will be yelling for her breakfast in a minute."

Abigail never forgot that birthday. It was a beautiful day, and they went for a walk along the lane. Aiden pushed the pram and Abigail held Sam's lead. The grass verges were lush and green, and wild flowers peeped at the little family as they passed.

Archie Draper saw them go by from a distance and smiled, making a mental note to tell Emily that all seemed well with the Martins.

Aiden cooked a romantic meal for two

that evening. He poured sparkling champagne into glasses.

"To us, and the future," he said.

"To us," said Abigail, raising her glass.

Their eyes locked.

That night they shared a bed for the first time in months.

16

When no more postcards plopped onto the doormat during the following weeks, Aiden dared to hope that Martha had lost interest and would no longer harass him.

Life was good. Tiffany was thriving, and Abigail was beginning to regain her sparkle. The wound that Aiden had inflicted was deep, but she was healing.

Then one dark day, another postcard landed on the mat. A garish photo of Times Square stared up at him. Aiden picked it up, shuddering, and read the message on the back. This time it was a little longer.

I've made my decision. I'm coming to collect the brat. Be warned, no court in the US or UK would come between a baby and its real mother.

Aiden's face was ashen. The thought of losing his baby daughter was unbearable. Should he warn Abigail and risk breaking her heart again? With a trembling hand, he placed the postcard with the others, hidden in his desk drawer.

Next day, another arrived, a picture of Brooklyn Bridge on the front.

I've booked the flight. I'll hire a car at Gatwick and drive down to Ten Cent Dump. See ya!

Aiden needed advice and made a decision. He dialled Stan Cooper's number at the police station.

"Morning, Stan. Aiden Martin here. I wonder whether I could pop down and see you for a chat? Something's come up and I would really appreciate your advice."

"Morning Mr Martin. Of course! Is it official business, or just friendly advice? I only ask because if it's informal, instead of going to the police station, knock on our kitchen door and Sally will make us a cuppa. Sometimes three heads are better than two."

"It's just friendly advice I need, and a cup of tea would be nice, thank you. It's about Tiffany."

Plucking the postcards from his drawer, he slipped them into his inside jacket pocket and called to Abigail who was upstairs with Tiffany.

"Abs, I'm going to walk down to the village to post a letter. Do you want anything?"

"No, thanks, don't think so. I'm going to try to have a tidy up here, otherwise Hilary will be very shocked when she comes back to start cleaning again next week. We'll see you later."

Aiden sat at the kitchen table with Stan and Sally Cooper.

"I took the liberty of filling Sally in on all

the details," said Stan. "I hope you don't mind."

Aiden shook his head.

"How is that little baby of yours?" asked Sally, smiling.

"She's gorgeous, thank you, growing fast. Abigail is a fantastic mother. But the reason I've come is this..."

He drew out the postcards and handed them to Stan one by one, in the order in which they had arrived.

"They're from Martha, of course. Tiffany's real mother."

Stan looked at each card, front and back, then passed them to his wife, who gasped.

"You see, I don't know if she's telling the truth, or just trying to frighten me to get more money out of me."

"She certainly doesn't sound very motherly," remarked Sally.

Stan laid the postcards in a row, end to end, and sat quietly thinking.

"But can she really take Tiffany away?" asked Aiden.

"Surely she can't," said Sally. "Can she, Stan?"

Stan took a deep breath.

"Here's what I think, for what it's worth. I think Martha is probably trying to scare you into offering her more money. If that's the case, you mustn't pay her because it'll never stop. She'll always be asking you for more money."

Sally and Aiden nodded.

"However, let's say that, after all, she's genuinely decided she wants to be a mother and take Tiffany back. I'm afraid it's possible that she *could* claim the baby. But she can't just turn up and knock on your door and expect you to hand over the baby. These things take time and have to be done officially. There'll be DNA checks and paperwork to complete. Maybe even a court case."

"You did well keeping these postcards," said Sally, tapping the cards on the table. "They may be used as evidence later."

"I suggest this," continued Stan. "Keep me informed of everything. If any more postcards arrive, tell me straight away. And if she turns up, *don't* let her in, just call me immediately."

"Should I tell Abigail, do you think?"

"Judging by these postcards, Martha is very unstable. If she writes again, yes, I think you should tell Abigail. I think it's only fair to warn her," said Sally.

Stan nodded in agreement.

"With any luck, Martha will just give up, and you won't hear any more," he said.

———

The next day, the sky was black and storm clouds rolled in. Torrential rain fell, leaving great puddles in the lane.

In spite of the terrible weather, the postman crunched up the drive to deliver the mail. A picture postcard dropped on the mat. It showed a picture of Big Ben, and bore an English first class stamp. Aiden's pulse raced as he picked it up.

Cooeee! I'm here! Gotten myself a car and should reach Ten Cent Dump tomorrow. Make sure the brat is ready.

Aiden checked the postmark. Yesterday!

That meant that Martha could arrive at any minute!

He raced to the phone and read the latest message out loud to Stan.

"Right," said Stan. "Make sure all your doors are locked. If anything happens, and I mean *anything,* inform me. And I think you should tell Mrs Martin."

Outside, the storm raged. Giant raindrops pounded the windows and lightning flashed in the sky. Aiden walked into the kitchen where Abigail was rocking Tiffany to sleep.

"Can you believe this weather?" she asked, staring through the window.

"Abs, I need to tell you something. I didn't want to, but it's important."

Abigail caught the urgency in his tone and looked up, concerned.

"What is it?"

So Aiden told her about the postcards, and his visit to Stan. He showed her the cards and saw her face blanche. He handed her the final postcard.

"The postmark means she's on her way now," he said.

Abigail's hand covered her mouth in shock.

"What shall we do?"

"Stan says we should lock all the doors. She can't take Tiffany, and we're not going to let her into the house. If she turns up, we phone the police."

Abigail's face was white, but her jaw had a determined set to it. She nodded, clutching Tiffany closer to her.

"I think you should take Tiffany upstairs, and I'll keep watch downstairs."

As he spoke, the sky flashed white, followed by a terrific clap of thunder that shook the house.

All the lights went out.

17

Aiden grabbed the flashlight from the drawer. Rain lashed the windows.

"Quick! Grab everything you might need and take Tiffany upstairs. I'll help you get settled then I'm going to wait down here. If that madwoman turns up, I'll be ready, storm or no storm. Let's hope the electricity comes back on soon."

When Abigail and Tiffany were safely installed upstairs, Aiden took up his station by the window, watching the rain bounce as it hit the ground. It was going to be a long day and night.

The hours ticked past and there was no sign of Martha. The rain never eased and the black clouds remained knitted together, blocking out any glimpse of the night sky. At around 3:00am, Aiden could keep his eyes open no longer. He slept fitfully in the chair by the window, but even as he slept he was listening for a car or footsteps on the gravel.

The electricity stayed off until morning. The ground was soaked and puddles glimmered under the grey sky, but the rain had stopped. Aiden tensed when he saw a figure approaching. He relaxed when he saw it was the postman who dropped two bills through the letterbox. No postcards.

Abigail came downstairs. She looked exhausted.

"Do you think Martha was lying?" she asked.

"I don't know…"

The phone rang and they both jumped.

"Stan here. Nothing to report?"

"No, nothing. I stayed on watch all night."

"Well, perhaps it was an empty threat. I suggest you get some rest, but keep your doors locked for the moment, just in case.

I've got my work cut out because of this storm, it's created havoc in the village. But I'll be here if you need me."

Aiden and Abigail tried hard to relax, but found it difficult. They talked endlessly about the possibility of Martha turning up, their eyes forever flicking to the window, their ears tuned in to the sound of any approaching car. To Aiden's relief, Abigail and he were united, utterly determined that Martha would never claim Tiffany.

Already worn out from being awake all night, every new noise alarmed them. They stared questioningly at each other, silently attempting to analyse the source of the sound. Their nerves jangled. When the paper boy wheeled his bike up the drive, they both nearly jumped out of their skins.

The phone rang again and Aiden picked it up.

"Hello?"

"Mr Martin? Stan Cooper here again. Have you had the Yewbridge Gazette yet?"

"Yes, it's just been delivered, this very minute. Why?"

"Do you have it there in front of you?

Look at the main story. I think you have nothing further to worry about." Stan rang off.

Aiden picked up the paper and smoothed it out. The whole of the front page was devoted to last night's storm.

Aiden stared at the main photo which showed the wreckage of a white car.

"Abigail! Look at this!"

"Oh my…"

Storm claims life of US tourist

Police have confirmed that the violent storms of yesterday have claimed the life of an American tourist. The driver appears to have lost control on a sharp bend between Yewbridge and Sixpenny Cross. There were no witnesses.

A police spokesman said, "The accident was reported by a motorist at 4:00pm yesterday. The car must have swerved off the road in the bad weather and hit a tree. The driver was pronounced dead on arrival at Yewbridge Hospital. Our enquiries show that the car was hired at Gatwick Airport by a Miss Martha

Guttman. A passport has been found and a positive identification has been made.

Miss Guttman's family in New York have been informed. Miss Guttman was not married and leaves no children."

Police have asked the public to continue to be aware of dangerous driving conditions caused by the storm.

"Abs, it's over… It's finally over."

Husband and wife fell into each other's arms. They stood entwined for a long time.

The next day, the sun shone on the village of Sixpenny Cross. The pond on the village green was fuller than anybody remembered it. The ducks' nest had been washed away, but the eggs had already hatched and the ducklings were safe and well. A tree had been struck by lightning in Sixpenny Woods, and the church had lost a few slates. Branches and debris needed to be cleared. Apart from that, there was not too much damage.

That evening, Aiden smiled into his wife's eyes across the restaurant table in Yewbridge. They must have passed the spot where Martha had spun off the road, but they hadn't looked for it.

"Well, this is a nice surprise," said Abigail. "I can't remember when we last went out to dinner together! It was good of Daisy to babysit at such short notice."

"I thought we should celebrate. I know we didn't wish Martha dead, but it's wonderful to know that nobody can ever take Tiffany away from us now."

The tiny diamonds in Abigail's eternity ring sparkled in the candlelight as she put her hand over his.

"Yes," she said, looking directly into his eyes, unblinking. "Especially since Tiffany is going to have a little brother or sister in a few months."

Aiden's eyes widened.

"Really?" he breathed.

"Yes, really."

Stan Cooper was enjoying a quiet pint in the Dew Drop. Actually, it was his second but he felt he deserved it. The Captain and his friend sat in their usual corner, and Bella Tait occupied another table, reading the Yewbridge Gazette and stroking Scout, the pub cat.

"Terrible storm, wasn't it?" said Angus, buffing up the beer taps and making conversation from behind the bar. "That poor American woman who crashed her car! What bad luck. I wonder where she was heading?"

"Dunno," said Stan, shaking his head.

"And I hear that nice Martin couple are keeping that baby that was found in the woods?"

"Yes, I heard that too," said Stan, and took a long sip of his beer.

18

*S*o you see, my dear, Abigail's story had a happy ending. She and Aiden went on to have lots more children. Abigail always wanted to fill that house in Sixpenny Lane with children, and over the years, that's exactly what she did. There wasn't one room in that house that wasn't bursting at the seams with kids, toys and laughter.

Of course, the children soon rubbed off the house's 'designer shine' and it began to look much more like a home, and less like a photo from *Country Estates* magazine. It began to look rather like the Drapers' farmhouse, cosy and rather worn round the edges. And Abigail and Aiden were very comfortable with that.

Aiden worked from home most of the time, and wore jeans with holes in them, only changing into his tailored suit when he had to go up to London on business. Money was not important to either him or Abigail. They lived for their children.

The children went to the village school across the green, which is where you will go when you're bigger. You'll like it there, and your teacher will take you on nature study trips across the green, and you'll catch little creatures with your net in the pond.

Perhaps if Martha had been a nicer person, none of this would have happened. Nobody wanted her dead, of course, but she kind of brought it on herself.

Just one little thing puzzled me and Jayne Fairweather, the postmistress, about Martha Guttman's death. You see, Jayne was the motorist who reported the accident to the police, so she was probably the first one on the scene.

She was driving back from Yewbridge to Sixpenny Cross, and she said the rain was bucketing down so hard she could scarcely see the road ahead. When she rounded the bend and caught sight of Martha's car wrapped round a tree, she stopped straight away, and rolled down her window. She realised it was extremely serious, but as she prepared to drive away to report the incident, a movement caught her eye.

She thought she saw two figures melting into the trees.

She told me it looked like an old lady with a shawl over her head, holding the hand of a small pale-faced child.

When she looked again, they'd gone, so she probably imagined it.

It's good to see you fast asleep with not a care in the world, little one. Next time I'm asked to watch over you, I'll tell you another story. Sixpenny Cross is bursting with stories.

I know you love animals, so I'm going to tell you all about Bella Tait.

Yes, _B is for Bella_. And Bella Tait's love of animals, big and small, scaly or fluffy, was a joy to behold.

But kind, loving, generous Bella didn't

know she had a mortal enemy.

ABIGAIL MARTIN'S CARROT CAKE

"Abigail, sorry to be a pest, but can you give me that carrot cake recipe again, please? I can't find it and I've searched everywhere."

INGREDIENTS

- Olive oil, to grease
- 2 (about 300g) carrots
- 1 cup (150g) self-raising flour
- ½ cup (75g) plain flour
- 1 teaspoon bicarbonate of soda
- ½ teaspoon ground cinnamon
- ½ cup (80g) brown sugar
- ¾ cup (185ml) olive oil
- ½ cup (125ml) golden syrup

- 3 eggs
- 1 teaspoon vanilla essence
- 250g (8oz) spreadable cream cheese
- ½ cup (80g) icing sugar
- ½ teaspoon vanilla essence

METHOD

- Preheat oven to 170C or 150C fan-assisted, or 340F.
- Grease a 20cm (8in) round cake pan lightly with oil, and line with non-stick baking paper.
- Peel and grate the carrots, and set aside.
- Sift the flours, bicarbonate of soda and cinnamon into a large bowl.
- Put the brown sugar, oil, golden syrup, eggs and vanilla in a separate bowl. Use a balloon whisk to mix until combined.
- Pour the oil mixture into the dry ingredients. Use a wooden spoon to stir gently until just combined. Stir in the grated carrot.
- Pour the mixture into the pan and bake for 1 hour. Set aside for 5

minutes, before turning out onto a wire rack to cool completely.

TO MAKE THE ICING

- Place the cream cheese, icing sugar and vanilla in a bowl. Use a wooden spoon to mix until well combined.
- Spread the icing over the cake.

A REQUEST...

We authors absolutely rely on our readers' reviews. We love them even more than a glass of chilled wine on a summer's night beneath the stars.

Even more than chocolate.

If you enjoyed this book, I'd be so grateful if you left a review, even if it's simply one sentence. It's the very best way for authors to get their books noticed.

THANK YOU!

PREVIEW OF CHICKENS, MULES AND TWO OLD FOOLS

BY VICTORIA TWEAD

If you enjoyed the Sixpenny Cross series, please join Victoria and Joe in the bestselling, awardwinning Old Fools series. This true story and series starter is *Chickens, Mules and Two Old Fools*.

PREVIEW

1

THE FIVE YEAR PLAN

"Hello?"

"This is Kurt."

"Oh! Hello, Kurt. How are you?"

"I am vell. The papers you vill sign now. I haf made an appointment vith the Notary for you May 23rd, 12 o'clock."

"Right, I'll check the flights and…" but he had already hung up.

Kurt, our German estate agent, was the type of person one obeyed without question. So, on May 23rd, we found ourselves back in Spain, seated round a huge polished table in the Notary's office. Beside us sat our bank manager holding a briefcase stuffed with bank notes.

Nine months earlier, we had never met Kurt. Nine months earlier, Joe and I lived in an ordinary house, in an ordinary Sussex town. Nine months earlier we had ordinary jobs and expected an ordinary future.

Then, one dismal Sunday, I decided to change all that.

"…heavy showers are expected to last through the Bank Holiday weekend and into next week. Temperatures are struggling to reach 14 degrees…"

August, and the weather-girl was wearing a coat, sheltering under an umbrella. June had been wet, July wetter. I sighed, stabbing the 'off' button on the remote control before she could depress me further. Agh! Typical British weather.

My depression changed to frustration. The private thoughts that had been tormenting me so long returned. Why should we put up with it? Why not move? Why not live in my beloved Spain where the sun always shines?

I walked to the window. Raindrops like slug trails trickled down the windowpane. Steely clouds hung low, heavy with more rain, smothering the town. Sodden litter sat drowning in the gutter.

"Joe?" He was dozing, stretched out on the sofa, mouth slightly open. "Joe, I want to talk to you about something."

Poor Joe, my long-suffering husband. His gangly frame was sprawled out, newspaper slipping from his fingers. He was utterly relaxed, blissfully unaware that our lives were about to change course.

How different he looked in scruffy jeans

compared with his usual crisp uniform. But to me, whatever he wore, he was always the same, an officer and a gentleman. Nearing retirement from the Forces, I knew he was looking forward to a tension-free future, but the television weather-girl had galvanised me into action. The metaphorical bee in my bonnet would not be stilled. It buzzed and grew until it became a hornet demanding attention.

"Huh? What's the matter?" His words were blurred with sleep, his eyes still closed. Rain beat a tattoo on the window pane.

"Joe? Are you listening?"

"Uhuh…"

"When you retire, I want us to sell up and buy a house in Spain." Deep breath.

There. The bomb was dropped. I had finally admitted my longing. I wanted to abandon England with its ceaseless rain. I wanted to move permanently to Spain.

Sleep forgotten, Joe pulled himself upright, confusion in his blue eyes as he tried to read my expression.

"Vicky, what did you say just then?" he asked, squinting at me.

"I want to go and live in Spain."

"You can't be serious."

"Yes, I am."

Of course it wasn't just the rain. I had plenty of reasons, some vague, some more solid.

I presented my pitch carefully. Our children, adults now, were scattered round the world; Scotland, Australia and London. No grandchildren yet on the horizon and Joe only had a year before he retired. Then we would be free as birds to nest where we pleased.

And the cost of living in Spain would be so much lower. Council tax a fraction of what we usually paid, cheaper food, cheaper houses... The list went on.

Joe listened closely and I watched his reactions. Usually, *he* is the impetuous one, not me. But I was well aware that his retirement fantasy was being threatened. His dream of lounging all day in his dressing-gown, writing his book and diverting himself with the odd mathematical problem was being exploded.

"Hang on, Vicky, I thought we had it all planned? I thought you would do a few days of supply teaching if you wanted, while I start writing my book." Joe absentmindedly scratched his nether regions. For once I ignored his infuriating habit; I was in full flow.

"But imagine writing in Spain! Imagine sitting outside in the shade of a grapevine and writing your masterpiece."

Outside, windscreen wipers slapped as cars swept past, tyres sending up plumes of filthy water. Joe glanced out of the window at the driving rain and I sensed I had scored an important point.

"Why don't you write one of your famous lists?" he suggested, only half joking.

I am well known for my lists and records. Inheriting the record- keeping gene from my father, I can't help myself. I make a note of the weather every day, the temperature, the first snowdrop, the day the ants fly, the exchange rate of the euro, everything. I make shopping lists, separate ones for each shop. I make To Do lists and 'Joe, will you please' lists. I make packing lists before holidays. I even make lists of lists. My nickname at work was Schindler.

So I set to work and composed what I considered to be a killer pitch:

- Sunny weather
- Cheap houses
- Live in the country
- Miniscule council tax
- Friendly people
- Less crime
- No heating bills
- Cheap petrol
- Wonderful Spanish food
- Cheap wine and beer
- Could get satellite TV so you won't miss English football
- Much more laid-back life style
- Could afford house big enough for family and visitors to stay
- No TV licence
- Only short flight to UK

- Might live longer because
  Mediterranean diet is healthiest in
  the world

When I ran dry, I handed the list to Joe. He glanced at it and snorted.

"I'm going to make a coffee," he said, but he took my list with him. He was in the kitchen a long time.

When he came out, I looked up at him expectantly. He ignored me, snatched a pen and scribbled on the bottom of the list. Satisfied, he threw it on the table and left the room. I grabbed it and read his additions. He'd pressed so hard with the pen that he'd nearly gone through the paper.

Joe had written:

- CAN'T SPEAK SPANISH!
- TOO MANY FLIES!
- *MOVING HOUSE IS THE PITS!*

For weeks we debated, bouncing arguments for and against like a game of ping pong. Even when we weren't discussing it, the subject hung in the air between us, almost tangible. Then one day, (was it a coincidence that it was raining yet again?) Joe surprised me.

"Vicky, why don't you book us a holiday over Christmas, and we could just take a look."

The hug I gave him nearly crushed his ribs.

"Hang on!" he said, detaching himself and holding me at arm's length. "What I'm trying to say is, well, I'm willing to compromise."

"What do you mean, 'compromise'?"

"How about if we look on it as a five year plan? We don't sell this house, just rent it out. Okay, we could move to Spain, but not necessarily for ever. At the end of five years, we can make up our minds whether to come back to England or stay out there. I'm happy to try it for five years. What do you think?"

I turned it over in my mind. Move to Spain, but look on it as a sort of project? Actually, it seemed rather a good idea. In fact, a perfect compromise.

Joe was watching me. "Well? Agreed?"

"Agreed…" It was a victory of sorts. A Five Year Plan. Yes, I saw the sense in that. Anything could happen in five years.

"Well, go on, then. Book a holiday over Christmas and we'll take it from there."

So I logged onto the Internet and booked a two week holiday in Almería.

Why Almería? Well, we already knew the area quite well as this would be our fourth visit. And I considered this part of Andalucía to be perfect. Only two and a half hours flight from London, guaranteed sunshine, friendly people and jaw-dropping views. It ticked all my boxes. Joe agreed cautiously that the area could be ideal.

So the destination was decided, but what type of home in Spain would we want? Our budget was reduced because we weren't going to sell our English house. We'd have to find something cheap.

On previous visits, I'd hated all the houses we'd noticed in the resorts. Mass produced boxes on legoland estates, each identical, each characterless and overlooking the next. No, I knew what I really wanted: a house we could do up, with views and space, preferably in an unspoiled Spanish village.

Unlike Joe, I've always been obsessed with houses. I was the driving force and it was the hard climb up the English property ladder that allowed us even to contemplate moving abroad. In the past few years, we had bought a derelict house, improved and sold it, making a good profit. So we bought another and repeated the process. It was gruelling work. We both had other careers, but it was well worth the effort. Now we could afford to rent out our home in England and still buy a modest house in Spain.

"If we do decide to move out there," said Joe, "and we buy an old place to do up, it's not going to be like doing up houses in England. Everything's going to be different there."

How right he was.

Like a child, I yearned for that Christmas to come. I couldn't wait to set foot on Spanish soil again. We arrived, and although Christmas lights decorated the airport, it was warm enough to remove our jackets. Before long, we had found our hotel and settled in.

The next morning, we hired a little car. Joe, having finally accepted the inevitable, was happy to drive into the mountains in search of The House. We had two weeks to find it.

Yet again the mountains seduced us. The endless blue sky where birds of prey wheeled lazily. The neat orchards splashed with bright oranges and lemons. The secret, sleepy villages nestled into valleys. Even the roads, narrow, treacherous and winding, couldn't break the spell that Andalucía cast over us.

Daily, we drove through whitewashed villages where little old ladies dressed in black stopped sweeping their doorsteps to watch us pass. We waved at farmers working in their fields, the dry dust swirling in irritated clouds from their labours. We paused to allow goat-herds to pass with their flocks, the lead goat's bell clanging bossily as the herd followed, snatching mouthfuls of vegetation on the run.

Although we hadn't yet found The House, we were positive we'd found the area we wanted to live in.

One day we drove into a village that clung to the steep mountainside by its fingernails. We entered a bar that was buzzing with activity. It was busy and the air heavy with smoke. The white-aproned bartender looked us up and down and jerked his head in greeting. No smile, just a nod.

Joe found a rocky wooden table by the window with panoramic views and we settled ourselves, soaking in the atmosphere. Four old men played cards at the next table. A heated debate was taking place between another group. I caught the words 'Barcelona' and 'Real Madrid'. Most of the bar's customers were male.

Grumpy, the bartender, wiped his hands on his apron and approached our table, flicking off imaginary crumbs from the surface with the back of his hand. He had a splendid moustache which concealed any expression he may have had, and made communication difficult.

"Could we see the menu, please?" asked Joe in his best phrase book Spanish.

Grumpy shook his head and snorted. It seemed there was no menu.

"No importa," said Joe. "It doesn't matter."

Using a combination of sign language and impatient grunts, Grumpy took our order but our meal was destined to be a surprise. A basket of bread was slammed onto the table, followed by two plates of food. Garlic mushrooms - delicious. We cleaned our plates and leaned back, digesting our food and the surroundings. In typical Spanish fashion, the drinkers at the bar bellowed at each other as though every individual had profound hearing problems.

"We're running out of time," said Joe. "We can carry on gallivanting around the countryside, but we aren't going to find anything. I very much doubt we'll find a house this holiday."

Suddenly, clear as cut crystal, the English

words, "Oh, bugger! Where are my keys?" floated above the Spanish hubbub.

Book #4

Two Old Fools in Spain Again

Life refuses to stand still in tiny El Hoyo. Lola Ufarte's behaviour surprises nobody, but when a millionaire becomes a neighbour, the village turns into a battleground.

Book #5

Two Old Fools in Turmoil

When dark, sinister clouds loom, Victoria and Joe find themselves facing life-changing decisions. Happily, silver linings also abound. A fresh new face joins the cast of well-known characters but the return of a bad penny may be more than some can handle.

Book #6

Two Old Fools Down Under

When Vicky and Joe wave goodbye to their beloved Spanish village, they face their future in Australia with some trepidation. Now they must build a new life amongst strangers, snakes and spiders the size of saucers. Accompanied by their enthusiastic new puppy, Lola, adventures abound, both heartwarming and terrifying.

Book #7

Two Old Fools Fair Dinkum

Life is good. The grandchildren are thriving despite swallowing magnets and sticking crayons up their noses. But after a terrible drought, bushfire season arrives early, and flames rage across the land. Will love and laughter be enough to keep the Two Old Fools and their family safe from harm?

Book #8

Two Old Fools Find Their Tribe

One Young Fool in Dorset (PREQUEL)

This light and charming story is the delightful prequel to Victoria Twead's Old Fools series. Her childhood memories are vividly portrayed, leaving the reader chuckling and enjoying a warm sense of comfortable nostalgia.

One Young Fool in South Africa (PREQUEL)

Who is Joe Twead? What happened before Joe met Victoria and they moved to a crazy Spanish mountain village? Joe vividly paints his childhood memories despite constant heckling from Victoria at his elbow.

NEW! THE STILLWATER MURDERS BY VICTORIA TWEAD

DEAD OF NIGHT SERIES BOOK 1

THE STILLWATER MURDERS

Stillwater Cove is a town built on quiet.

When a string of unexplained deaths shatters the calm of Stillwater Cove, detective Lara Lennox is sent from Sydney to investigate. Each victim is found carefully posed, a small paper star left behind.

The Stillwater Murders (Chapter 1)

This is my time.

I am calm, but ready, prepared.

The dead of night, when the world exhales and falls utterly still. When darkness gathers like a velvet tide, drawn quietly over the earth. The sky becomes an ink-deep ocean without horizon or seam. A place where the stars seem to hesitate before shining. Even the gulls tuck their heads beneath their wings and stay quiet, surrendering to the dark.

There is a moment just before dawn, when the world forgets to breathe. The sea holds still. The reeds stop whispering.

I wait for that moment.

It is the best time a person can cross from this life to the next without struggle. Without fear. Without the burden of the weight of the world pressing in behind their ribs.

The old woman couldn't sleep. She sits on her veranda swing, wrapped in a faded, knitted shawl.

Her eyes are closed, her hair silvered by the moon.

I've been watching her. She didn't see me. I heard her trying to hum a tune she no longer remembered.

Her voice trembled.

Her hands trembled.

Her soul trembled.

But not now.

Now she is still. Perfectly still. Her heart no longer beats.

Now she is beautiful in her quietness.

I kneel beside her, careful not to disturb the blanket tucked around her knees. A faint night breeze lifts a strand of hair from her cheek, and I smooth it gently back into place.

Warm. Soft.

She earned this.

She carried her burden for so long that the weight bent her shoulders. No one noticed how tired she had become.

But I noticed. I always notice.

There is no fear in her face. Only the softness and peace that comes when the world finally releases you, lets you go.

I take the small, red paper star from my pocket.

It is imperfect. Torn by my fingers. A little crooked at the edges. The first star I ever made was for her, the woman who taught me how to say goodbye.

I place it gently under the old woman's hand, letting it rest on the shawl.

I breathe in.

A new beginning always starts with a quiet ending.

I stay with her until the light begins to rise behind the drowned forest.

Until the world remembers to breathe again.

Then I stand.

Gently close her eyes.

And leave her to her peace.

No one should die alone.

Amazon Link: https://bit.ly/Stillwater-Murders

REVIEWS

"I'm going: 'Nooooo! Don't go out, lock your door, don't let anyone in!' If this was TV I would be shouting at the screen."

"Totally wowed with it!"

"A brilliant edge-of-your-seat read."

"Totally and utterly gripping. I got nothing done while reading this."

NEW! THE BONE GARDEN BY VICTORIA TWEAD

DEAD OF NIGHT SERIES BOOK 2

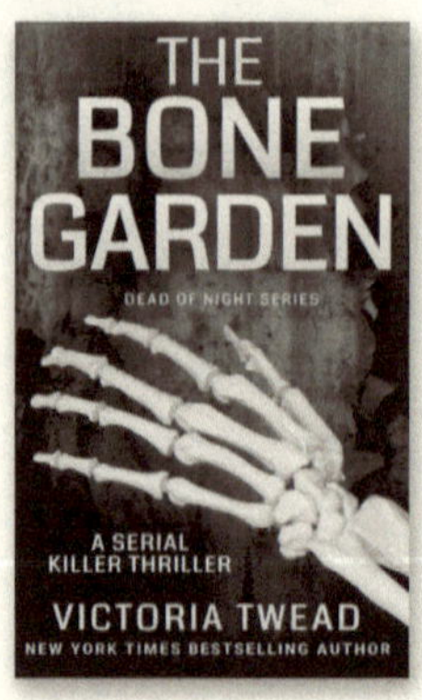

THE BONE GARDEN

Some patterns should never be completed.

Bodies are turning up, posed with impossible care, surrounded by spirals built from bleached bones.

Detective Senior Constable Lara Lennox expects a straightforward hunt. Instead, she finds a killer who seems to know her team's next move before they do.

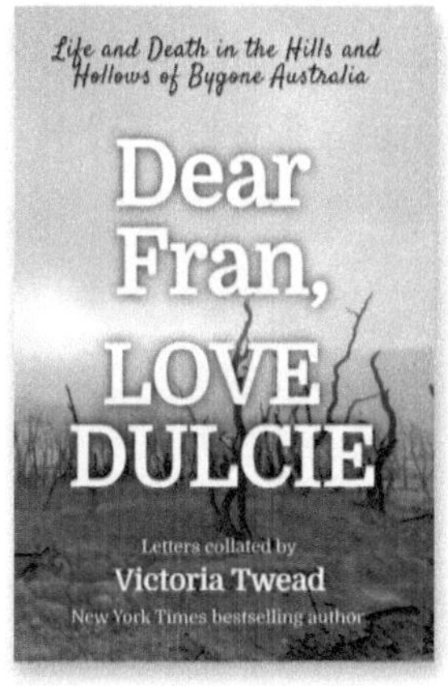

Dear Fran, Love Dulcie is a true story, a rollercoaster read, with *an unguessable, astonishing ending*. It will inform you, surprise you, reduce you to tears and haunt you forever. I've never quite been the same since Dulcie's life touched mine. I'm deeply humbled to have been asked to put the story together for the world to enjoy.

"Shocking, yet heart-warming. Overwhelmingly

gripping." Beth Haslam, author of the Fat Dogs and French Estates series.

"Wow! Goosebumps." Elizabeth Moore, author of the Someday Travels series and Top 1000 Amazon reviewer.

"A truly remarkable young woman and a unique record of Australian life." Valerie Poore, author of Watery Ways.

"There are no words that can do this book justice." Julie Haigh, Top 1000 Amazon reviewer.

ABOUT THE AUTHOR

Victoria Twead is the New York Times bestselling author of *Chickens, Mules and Two Old Fools* and the subsequent books in the Old Fools series. She is also the founder of Ant Press and the popular Facebook group, We Love Memoirs.

After living in a remote mountain village in Spain for eleven years, and owning probably the most dangerous cockerel in Europe, Victoria and Joe retired to Australia to watch their new grandchildren thrive amongst kangaroos and koalas.

More joyous life-chapters are unwinding.

For photographs and additional unpublished material to accompany this book,

download the
Free Photo Book from
www.victoriatwead.com/free-stuff

CONTACTS AND LINKS

CONNECT WITH VICTORIA

Email: TopHen@VictoriaTwead.com (emails welcome)
Website: www.VictoriaTwead.com
Old Fools' Updates Signup:
www.VictoriaTwead.com
This includes the latest Old Fools' news, free books, book recommendations, and recipe. Guaranteed spam-free and sent out every few months.
Free Stuff: http://www.victoriatwead.com/Free-Stuff/
Facebook: https://www.facebook.com/VictoriaTwead (friend requests welcome)
Instagram: @victoria.twead
Victoria's Cut-Price Paperback Bookstore: Books.by/Victoria-Twead

We Love Memoirs

Join me and other memoir authors and readers in the We Love Memoirs Facebook group, the friendliest group on Facebook. www.facebook.com/groups/welovemem oirs/

VICTORIA'S BOOKSTORE

BOOKSTORE LINK:
BOOKS.BY/VICTORIA-TWEAD

If you prefer to read paperbacks, and would like to pay lower prices by buying direct, do visit Victoria's own cut-price bookstore. Shipping anywhere in the world is a flat fee of $5.

Scan me

MORE ANT
PRESS MEMOIRS

AWESOME AUTHORS
~ AWESOME BOOKS

If you enjoyed this book, you may also enjoy these other Ant Press memoir authors. All titles are available in ebook, paperback, hardback and large print editions from **Amazon**.

**These two booksellers offer FREE delivery worldwide.
Blackwells.co.uk and Wordery.com
More Stores
Waterstones (Europe delivery),
Booktopia (Australia), Barnes & Noble
(USA), and all good bookstores.**

**VICTORIA TWEAD
New York Times bestselling author
The Old Fools series**

1.Chickens, Mules and Two Old Fools
2.Two Old Fools ~ Olé!
3.Two Old Fools on a Camel
4.Two Old Fools in Spain Again
5.Two Old Fools in Turmoil
6.Two Old Fools Down Under
7.Two Old Fools Fair Dinkum
8.Two Old Fools Find their Tribe
8.One Young Fool in Dorset (Prequel)
9.One Young Fool in South Africa (Prequel)

Dear Fran, Love Dulcie: Life and Death in the Hills and Hollows of Bygone Australia

BETH HASLAM
The Fat Dogs series

Fat Dogs and French Estates ~ Part I
Fat Dogs and French Estates ~ Part II
Fat Dogs and French Estates ~ Part III
Fat Dogs and French Estates ~ Part IV
Fat Dogs and French Estates ~ Part V
Fat Dogs and French Estates ~ Part VI
Fat Dogs and Welsh Estates ~ The Prequel

DIANE ELLIOTT
Lady Goatherder series

Butting Heads in Spain: Lady Goatherder 1
El Maestro: Lady Goatherder 2

EJ BAUER
The Someday Travels series

1.From Moulin Rouge to Gaudi's City
2.From Gaudi's City to Granada's Red
Palace
3.From an Umbrian Farmhouse to Como's
Quiet Shores

For more information about stockists, Ant Press titles or how to publish with Ant Press, please visit our website or contact us by email.

WEBSITE: www.antpress.org

EMAIL: admin@antpress.org

9 781922 476036